No Horizon:

Survivor's Edge

by Ed Rodriguez

Ed Rodriguez

No Horizon: Survivor's Edge

For permission requests, write to the author at:
Ed Rodriguez
Edgd00@hotmail.com

ISBN: 979-8-9928580-0-6

Cover design: Neil Que
Interior design: Ed Rodriguez

Printed in the United States of America

First Edition: 2025

Dedication

For my son, **Xavier,** I am immensely proud of you and love you deeply. This book is dedicated to you, as a testament to the pride I feel and the bond we share.

For my brother, **Axel**, who has always been an example of a good and honorable man. Your integrity and strength have guided me more than you know.

For my sister **Carmen** and my mother **Marita**, the strongest women I have ever known, who raised me to be a strong but empathetic man. Your resilience and unwavering love have shaped who I am today.

For all the strong women who have graced my life, family, friends, partners, and those who have come and gone— each of you has left an imprint on my heart and mind. Your strength, wisdom, and courage continue to inspire me.

And for all those who live everyday with trauma and emotional wounds, fighting a silent battle that few can see. Your courage to continue is a triumph that deserves recognition. You are not alone.

Acknowledgements

Writing "No Horizon: Survivor's Edge" has been a journey, and I couldn't have completed it without the support and encouragement of many incredible people.

To my friends and family who have believed in me even when I didn't—your unwavering support has meant the world to me. Thank you for standing by me through every challenge and triumph.

Special thanks to my beta readers whose invaluable feedback and insights have helped shape this book into what it is today. Your thoughtful critiques and encouragement made all the difference.

Lastly, to my readers and the wonderful community of supporters—your enthusiasm and encouragement have been a constant source of motivation. This book is for you.

Thank you all for being part of this journey.

Table of Contents

An Important Note to Readers:

The **Foreword** and **Afterword** contain important context about the intentional structure and approach of these stories. While each story stands alone, understanding the overarching vision may enhance your reading experience.

The **Foreword** provides essential framing before you begin, while the **Afterword** offers deeper insights into the themes and psychology explored throughout the collection.

Foreword

When I first began imagining the world of No Horizon, I was haunted by a single question: Who do we become when everything familiar is stripped away?

This isn't a story about heroes. Heroes belong to a world with clear lines between right and wrong. But in the wasteland of No Horizon, those lines have long since blurred into survival's gray dawn. Here, morality is a luxury, and the only certainty is the relentless grind of existence.

Instead, I wanted to craft a survivor whose strength isn't superhuman but entirely human—forged in the crucible of necessity and honed through brutal experience. She has no name because she could be any of us. Her tactical mind and unflinching resolve aren't the qualities of someone destined for greatness, but of someone who refused to accept an end when the world offered nothing else.

What began as an action-driven anthology with familiar zombie apocalypse tropes evolved into something more complex. I set out to create stories filled with tactical survival, combat techniques, and the visceral thrill of navigating a world overrun by the infected. I wanted the satisfaction of those genre elements we all recognize—the tension of a well-executed ambush, the relief of a secure shelter, the triumph of outwitting both the dead and the living. But I also wanted to break conventions, to approach these familiar scenarios in ways as resourceful and unexpected as my protagonist would.

I initially envisioned her as a blank slate, but as I developed each story, she refused to remain merely a vehicle for action. With each decision, each moment of brutal clarity, she emerged with a presence and history I hadn't planned. I followed where she led, discovering her trauma and her reasons for persisting when surrender would have been easier. This journey reflected truths from my own experiences with depression—that we don't outgrow our wounds but learn to navigate life carrying them.

The stories in this collection unfold without chronological restraint, much like memories that surface according to their own logic rather than linear time. Each entry stands entirely on its own, requiring no previous knowledge to appreciate. Whether this is your first encounter with this world or your tenth, you can open to any story and find a complete experience. Read in any order, these stories collectively paint a mosaic—a nuanced portrait of the survivor emerging piece by piece through her experiences.

The writing style, with its deliberate repetition—of phrases, of tactical assessments, of survival routines—mirrors the psychological reality of extreme conditions. When life narrows to its essential components, language and thought similarly contract. The mechanical descriptions, the clinical cataloging of supplies and threats, the utilitarian prose—these aren't just stylistic choices but reflections of a mind focused entirely on continuation. In a world where tomorrow holds no guarantees, where isolated settlements rise and fall amid the ruins of civilization, where the infected roam barren landscapes, language becomes as essential and unadorned as any other survival tool.

You won't find a traditional hero's journey here. There is no promised redemption waiting at the end of trials. Our protagonist isn't moving toward some idealized version of herself. She is simply enduring, adapting, surviving—and these stories honor the raw truth that sometimes, the greatest victory is merely to continue existing in a world that offers no horizon to move toward.

What I hope readers find in these pages is not an escape from reality but a reflection of it—a reminder that survival isn't about extraordinary strength but extraordinary persistence. That even in a world stripped to its brutal foundations, strategy trumps force, patience overcomes panic, and the line between survival and savagery remains razor-thin.

The horizon may be gone, but in its absence we discover what truly matters: not where we're going, but how we continue moving forward when all direction is lost. Thank you for walking this wasteland with me.

—Ed Rodriguez

No Horizon: Lost Days

She woke to the sound of splintering wood. Dawn light filtered through the boarded windows of the sixth-floor apartment, casting long shadows across the cramped space. The barricade at the door was holding, but not for long. Her hand reached instinctively for the crowbar beside her sleeping bag.

Three infected had found her. Their ragged breathing and animalistic snarls echoed through the thin walls. She'd chosen this location because of the narrow hallway—a natural bottleneck. Now that tactical decision would be tested.

The door frame cracked. No time to pack properly. She slung her backpack over her shoulders and gripped the crowbar in her right hand, survival knife in her left. When the first infected burst through, she was ready.

Its bloodshot eyes locked onto her, pupils dilated with rage. It lunged forward with unnatural speed. She sidestepped, driving the pointed end of the crowbar through its temple with practiced efficiency. The infected dropped instantly. She planted her boot on its chest, extracting the crowbar with a wet sound.

The second infected was halfway through the doorway when she met it. The knife sliced across its outstretched hands, severing tendons. As it stumbled, she brought the crowbar down in an arc, crushing its skull against the doorframe.

The third came too quickly. It caught her sleeve, yellowish foam spraying from its mouth. Its teeth snapped inches from her face as she twisted away, the ragged nails scoring her jacket. She dropped the knife, grabbed the infected's throat with her free hand, and drove the crowbar through its eye socket with the other.

She turned her face away just in time as blood sprayed from the wound. She held her breath, waiting for the struggling to stop. When it did, she retrieved her knife and wiped both weapons clean on the infected's tattered clothing.

The commotion would draw more. She had minutes, not hours.

She gathered her sleeping bag, filled her water bottles, and checked her weapons. The pump action shotgun remained strapped to her pack, unfired. The handaxe and machete hung from her belt. Ammunition was too precious to waste on three infected when silence and steel would suffice.

The afternoon sun beat down as she traversed the remains of what had once been a suburban shopping district. She moved with purpose but without haste, conserving energy, staying close to buildings for cover. Her eyes constantly scanned rooftops and alleyways. The rabid were dangerous, but the recently dead ones —the reanimated—were worse. They moved slower but felt no pain and required precise brain trauma to stop. And then there were the raiders, the worst threat of all.

Water and shelter were today's priorities. Food could wait another day.

She spotted the pharmacy from two blocks away. Its windows were intact—unusual, and therefore suspicious. She watched for twenty minutes from behind an overturned postal van, observing patterns, looking for signs of habitation or traps. Nothing moved.

Approaching from the rear, she used the handaxe to force the back door, the metal head making minimal noise against the frame. Inside, she found what she expected—picked-over shelves, discarded packaging. But raiders were often careless. They took the obvious: narcotics, antibiotics, bandages. She searched methodically, finding salt tablets, water purification drops, and feminine hygiene products hidden behind toppled displays.

The crash from the front of the store made her drop instantly to a crouch. She drew the machete, its weight reassuring in her grip.

Around the corner, she saw it—a reanimated corpse in advanced decay, moving with the distinctive shuffling gait of the dead. Its lower jaw was missing, the flesh of its neck blackened with rot. One arm ended at the elbow, maggots visibly writhing in the exposed bone.

She circled behind it, moving silent as a shadow. When she struck, it was with surgical precision—the machete cleaving through the back of the skull, severing the brain stem. The corpse crumpled without a sound.

She wiped the blade on its clothing, checked the store once more for overlooked supplies, then moved on.

The rainstorm caught her an hour before sunset. She took shelter in an abandoned gas station, creating a defensive position behind the counter. Rain meant reduced visibility for all, but sound would carry differently. She'd need to be vigilant.

Using the crowbar, she pried open an access panel in the floor, revealing the maintenance space for the underground storage tanks. Dry and defensible, with only one way in. She lowered her pack and settled in to wait out the storm.

She ate sparingly—half a protein bar, a few strips of dried venison from a successful hunt a few days prior. She cleaned her weapons methodically, oiling the moving parts of the shotgun, sharpening the blade of the machete with a whetstone. She checked her map, planning tomorrow's route. The town's water treatment plant was five miles northeast. It would have tools, possibly chemicals for purification.

The sound came just after midnight. Not the random shambling of the dead or the frenetic movements of the infected, but the deliberate steps of the living. Raiders.

She counted three distinct patterns of footfalls. They were being cautious but were clearly unfamiliar with proper noise discipline. She chambered a round in the shotgun, the action deliberately audible.

"We know you're in there," a man's voice called. "We don't want trouble. Just trading."

She remained silent. Raiders never wanted to trade. They wanted to take.

"We've got medicine. Antibiotics. You sound like you're alone. It's not safe to be alone."

She pressed herself against the wall beside the access panel, shotgun aimed at the opening. Her left hand held the handaxe, ready.

The footsteps circled the building. A flashlight beam swept across the interior. Then came the sound of breaking glass.

The first raider dropped into her hiding space feet-first, confident and careless. The shotgun boomed in the confined space, the sound deafening. The raider's chest disappeared in a red mist. Before the echo faded, she was moving.

She swung up through the opening, handaxe leading. The second raider was still blinded by the muzzle flash. The axe caught him under the chin, driving upward. He fell backward without a sound.

The third raider was smarter. He fired wildly from behind a shelf, forcing her to drop flat. She heard him reloading. Slinging the shotgun, she drew the machete and crowbar, then rolled behind a fallen display.

"You crazy bitch!" he screamed. "We just wanted to help!"

She moved from cover to cover, circling toward his position. When he fired again, she counted the shots. Six. Revolver. When he paused to reload, she attacked from his flank.

The crowbar knocked the weapon from his hands. The machete opened his forearm to the bone as he raised it in defense. His scream cut short as she drove the pointed end of the crowbar through his throat.

She collected their weapons and ammunition with swift decisiveness. Their packs yielded unexpected treasures: half a bottle of powdered bleach, fishing line, a sewing kit, and most valuable of all, a squeeze bottle of honey. Natural antibiotic, wound treatment, and calorie-dense food all in one.

By dawn, she was five miles away, leaving no trail to follow.

The water treatment plant rose before her, surrounded by chain-link fence topped with barbed wire. Perfect for keeping out the mindless infected and shambling dead, but also perfect for trapping the unwary. She circled the perimeter twice before finding a section of fence where the soil had eroded, creating a space just wide enough to squeeze through.

Inside, she swept each building systematically. The main treatment room held a cluster of seven reanimated corpses, their flesh gray-green with algae from the flooded floor. Their waterlogged movements were sluggish.

She considered her options. The shotgun would be quick but loud. There was another way.

She retreated to an office building, finding a rolling chair and length of pipe. Outside, she banged the pipe against a metal

18

railing, then used the chair to reach higher ground on a catwalk. The dead followed the sound, shambling through the door she left open.

One by one, she dispatched them from above. The machete for the first three, the handaxe for two more when the blade began to dull. The final two received the crowbar, their skulls collapsing with wet crunches under its weight.

In the filtration building, she found what she sought—calcium hypochlorite, still sealed in its original containers. With this, she could purify water for months. She took only what she could carry comfortably, aware that being overburdened meant being slow, and slow meant dead.

As she prepared to leave, a familiar sound reached her ears—the distinctive wheezing breath of the infected. Not just one. Many.

Through broken windows, she saw them—at least twenty, running with that unnatural, rabid speed toward the plant. Someone or something had agitated them, sending them in her direction. No time for stealth now.

She slung her pack, checked her weapons, and plotted her escape route. The fence was too exposed. The infected would see her, and in open ground, their speed gave them the advantage. She needed another way.

The drainage culvert. It would be partially submerged, cold, and possibly home to the dead, but it led away from the oncoming horde.

She slipped into the icy water, suppressing a gasp at the temperature. The shotgun was held high above her head as she waded forward into the darkness of the tunnel. Behind her, the first infected breached the treatment plant, their howls echoing across the concrete.

The culvert narrowed as she progressed, the water rising to her chest. In the darkness ahead, something moved. The splashing was too regular to be current.

She holstered the shotgun and drew the machete. When the reanimated corpse lunged from the water, she was ready. The blade severed its outstretched arms at the elbows, then cleaved through its skull on the backswing. The body sank silently beneath the surface.

For half an hour, she fought her way through the flooded tunnel, dispatching three more waterlogged dead with mechanical precision. When she finally emerged from the drainage pipe, she was a mile from the treatment plant. The infected were nowhere to be seen.

She found high ground and made camp as the sun set, building a small, smokeless fire to dry her clothes and prevent hypothermia. Tomorrow would bring new challenges, new threats. She would face them as she had faced all others since the world ended.

With the patient, implacable resolve of one who understood that survival wasn't about being stronger or faster than the dead or the infected. It was about being smarter than the living.

Ed Rodriguez

No Horizon: No Safe Place

The farmhouse had stood for nearly a century before the world ended. It would serve her needs for exactly one night.

She approached from downwind, crouched low in the overgrown cornfield. The two-story structure stood silhouetted against the setting sun, windows dark and shuttered. No smoke from the chimney. No movement behind the glass. A rusted pickup sat in the gravel drive, listing to one side on rotted tires.

She watched for thirty minutes, noting the location of doors, estimating the thickness of walls, counting potential exit routes. Patience had kept her alive this long. Impatience had killed everyone else.

The shotgun remained slung across her back as she circled the property. The crowbar made less noise. When she finally approached the back door, the light was fading fast. She tested the handle—locked. Expected. She wedged the curved end of the crowbar into the doorjamb and applied pressure with mechanical precision. The wood splintered with a muted crack.

Inside, she swept each room with mechanical precision, crowbar held ready. The kitchen cabinets yielded nothing but mouse droppings and cobwebs. The living room held a moth-eaten sofa and a brick fireplace. Upstairs: three bedrooms, stripped bare long ago.

She chose the attic for her shelter. One way in, accessible via a pull-down ladder she could retract behind her. A dormer window offered a view of the approach to the house and an emergency exit to the roof. She spread her sleeping bag in the corner furthest from the window, where the roof's angle would hide any light.

Only after securing her position did she allow herself to eat—a handful of dried berries and half a protein bar. She drank precisely eight ounces of water from her canteen. Her supplies would last three more days if she rationed carefully.

The sound of a branch snapping outside froze her mid-chew. She extinguished her small light, moving silently to the window.

In the moonlight, she saw them—a pack of twelve infected moving with the jerky, uncoordinated gait of the recently turned. Their breathing was still labored, lungs not yet failed, bodies not yet dead enough to reanimate. They prowled the edge of the cornfield, heads swiveling in that distinctive predatory pattern, sniffing the air.

One suddenly broke from the group, sprinting toward the house with unnatural speed. It had caught her scent. Within seconds, the others followed, a wave of snarling hunger rushing toward her position.

She weighed her options with cold calculation. The shotgun would take down two, maybe three before the noise drew every infected within a mile. The attic was defensible, but she'd be trapped. Stealth had failed. Now came violence.

The first infected hit the back door at full sprint, crashing through the damaged frame. She heard them spread through the lower level, furniture splintering, glass breaking. Their guttural howls echoed up the stairwell.

She waited at the top of the attic ladder, handaxe in her right hand, knife in her left. When the first infected appeared at the bottom of the ladder, she remained motionless. Two more joined it, their bloodshot eyes scanning upward.

The lead infected began to climb, fingernails tearing against the wooden rungs. She let it ascend until its head cleared the opening, then struck with brutal efficiency. The handaxe buried itself between its eyes. It convulsed once, then went limp, hanging half in the attic.

She grabbed its belt, hauling the body upward to block the opening. The other infected clawed at their fallen packmate, trying to push past. She took three quick steps back, drew the shotgun, and waited.

When another infected managed to squeeze through, she fired once. The blast in the confined space was deafening. The infected's head disappeared in a red mist, the body tumbling back down the ladder, taking another with it.

No time to reload. She slung the shotgun, grabbed her pack, and moved to the window. The old roof creaked under her weight as she crawled out onto the shingles. Below, more infected circled the house, drawn by the gunshot.

She edged along the roof peak to the far side of the house. The drop was fifteen feet to hard ground—survivable but risky. A large oak stood twenty feet away, its sturdy branches reaching toward the house but falling short by a few feet.

The infected were inside now, their howls echoing from below as they searched for access to the attic. She had minutes at most.

Unslinging her pack, she removed a coil of paracord. She attached her crowbar to one end, creating a makeshift grappling hook. After two practice swings, she hurled it toward the nearest thick branch. The crowbar wrapped around twice, slipping before catching securely on a fork in the branch. She pulled the cord taut. It would have to do.

Securing her pack again, she wrapped the cord around her forearm and took a running start across the roof peak. She leapt from the edge, swinging in a wide arc toward the tree. The branch creaked ominously. The crowbar shifted. She released the cord at the apex of her swing, landing hard against a lower branch, her ribs taking the impact.

She clung there, breath knocked from her lungs, as the crowbar and cord clattered to the ground below. An infected on the ground spotted her, charging toward the tree. She recovered quickly, climbing higher into the oak's dense foliage.

From her new vantage point, she watched as the farmhouse became overrun. Infected poured from windows and doors, searching. Eventually, they would leave. Patience, again, would be her salvation.

By dawn, they had dispersed, pursuing other prey or returning to whatever dark places they inhabited during daylight. She descended cautiously, retrieving her crowbar and cord from where they had fallen. Her ribs ached from the impact, but nothing seemed broken.

She oriented herself by the rising sun and began walking west. Another shelter waited somewhere ahead. Another temporary refuge in a world that offered none.

The highway stretched before her, a cracked ribbon of asphalt choked with abandoned vehicles. She moved between them, stooping occasionally to check underneath for lurking dangers. The mid-day sun beat down mercilessly, the heat rippling off the road surface.

A gas station appeared on the horizon, its sign long since toppled. Beside it stood a small convenience store, windows intact but covered with dust. Too intact. She approached with heightened caution.

Three hundred yards out, she took cover behind a derelict semi-truck and observed. No movement inside. No tracks in the dust outside. The tactical part of her mind noted multiple entry points, flat roof access, and limited visibility from within—a potential trap, but also a potential resource cache.

She circled wide, approaching from behind. A chain-link fence surrounded a small storage area behind the building. Inside the fence, two propane tanks stood undisturbed. She tested the gate—locked with a simple padlock. The handaxe made short work of it.

The back door was secured with a heavy deadbolt. She considered her options, then moved to a small window near the door. Using the handle of the machete, she tapped lightly on the glass—testing for reaction. Nothing. She tapped again, louder.

A dark shape lunged against the glass from inside, cracking it. Not an infected—the movement was too slow, too uncoordinated. One of the reanimated dead. She could handle one.

She broke the window with the crowbar, then stepped back as decayed arms thrust through the opening. Using the machete, she severed both limbs at the elbows. The dead thing continued to press forward, unaffected by the loss. When its head emerged through the window, she brought the handaxe down with calculated force, splitting the skull.

The body slumped half in, half out of the window. She waited, listening for others. Silence.

Clearing the window frame of broken glass, she climbed through. The store's interior was surprisingly untouched—shelves still stocked with dust-covered packages. The scent of putrefaction hung in the stale air, emanating from a second corpse behind the counter. This one truly dead, a bullet hole in its temple, a revolver still clutched in its mummified hand.

She pried the weapon loose, checking its cylinder. One round fired, five remaining. She added it to her collection.

The store yielded unexpected bounty: canned goods, bottled water, batteries still in their packaging. Too much to carry. She would need to prioritize.

As she sorted through supplies, a sound outside froze her mid-motion—the unmistakable rumble of an engine. Humans. Raiders, most likely.

She moved swiftly to the front, peering through a gap in the dusty windows. A modified pickup truck approached, steel plates welded to its sides, barbed wire wrapped around the bumper. Three figures rode in the bed, armed with various weapons. Two more in the cab.

Five raiders. Too many to fight directly.

She retreated to the back room, gathering only what would fit in her pack—water purification tablets, antibiotic ointment, matches in waterproof containers. She shoved a can opener and a small bottle of iodine into her jacket pocket.

The truck engine died outside. Male voices called to each other as they approached the store. She had seconds, not minutes.

The dead store clerk gave her an idea. She positioned herself behind the counter, next to the desiccated corpse, the newly acquired revolver in hand. The machete lay across her lap.

The front door opened with a jingle of rusty bells. Two raiders entered, rifles sweeping the interior.

"Place looks untouched," one said. "Check the back."

"What about that?" the other replied, gesturing toward the counter where she hid with the corpse.

"Just another dead one."

Footsteps approached the counter. A face appeared above her—bearded, filthy, eyes widening in surprise as they met hers. Before he could shout, she fired the revolver upward through his jaw. The report echoed in the confined space.

She was moving before his body hit the floor, vaulting the counter as the second raider turned toward the noise. The machete caught him across the throat. He fired reflexively, the shot going wide, shattering a display of dusty snack foods.

Outside, the remaining raiders shouted in alarm. She grabbed the fallen raider's rifle—an old hunting model, lever action. Moving to the side of the window, she counted three figures taking cover behind their truck.

"Hank! Curtis!" one called. No response from inside.

A tense standoff followed. They couldn't rush the store without exposing themselves. She couldn't leave without crossing open ground.

"We just want to talk!" one raider shouted. "We can trade!"

The oldest trick. She didn't reply.

One raider made a dash toward the side of the building. She tracked him through the window, leading his movement, then fired once with the lever action. He stumbled, clutching his thigh, but made it to cover.

Four rounds left in the rifle. Five in the revolver. Two raiders unhurt, one wounded.

The sun was setting, shadows lengthening across the parking lot. Darkness would change the equation, giving her the advantage. She settled in to wait.

An hour passed. The raiders grew restless, whispering among themselves. One suddenly rose from behind the truck, firing wildly at the store. She pressed herself flat against the wall as bullets shattered the remaining windows.

In the commotion, she noticed the other raider attempting to circle behind the building. She moved quickly to the back room, positioning herself beside the broken window.

When he appeared, he was looking over his shoulder, distracted. The machete took his hand off at the wrist. His scream was cut short as she drove the blade through his neck.

Two left—one injured, one increasingly desperate.

Night had fallen completely now. She retrieved a bottle of cleaning fluid from beneath the counter, stuffing a rag into its neck. The Molotov cocktail was crude but effective. She lit it with a match and hurled it through the broken front window toward the truck.

The vehicle erupted in flames, illuminating the parking lot in flickering orange light. The unwounded raider broke cover, running for the tree line. She dropped him with a single shot from the rifle.

The wounded one remained hidden behind the burning truck, trapped between the fire and her position. She slung her pack, checked her weapons, and slipped out the back door.

Circling wide through the darkness, she approached from behind. He never saw her coming. The knife entered at the base of his skull, severing the brain stem. He collapsed without a sound.

She searched the bodies efficiently, taking only what was useful—ammunition, a compass, water purifiers, a roll of duct tape. By the time she finished, the truck was fully engulfed, a beacon visible for miles. Time to move on.

She headed west again, guided by starlight, leaving the burning gas station behind. The supplies she'd gathered would last weeks if properly rationed. The violence would draw infected and dead alike, but she would be long gone before they arrived.

In the distance, a water tower loomed against the night sky. Potential shelter, with high ground and visibility. She adjusted her course, already planning her approach, her defense, her eventual departure.

One more night of survival in a world that no longer allowed for anything else.

Ed Rodriguez

No Horizon: Shadow's Edge

She crouched behind the rusted remains of an overturned truck, counting breaths to steady her pulse. Three travelers moved along the cracked asphalt below, unaware of her position on the ridge. Their packs bulged with supplies – medicine perhaps, or ammunition, food certainly. Her own resources had dwindled to dangerous levels: four shotgun shells, half a canteen of water, and protein bars that wouldn't last another day.

The machete hung heavy at her side. One clean ambush. That's all it would take.

Her fingers tightened around the weapon's handle as she calculated angles of approach, estimating the travelers' reaction times. The tallest one limped slightly – easy target first. The woman in the middle carried a rifle but kept it slung too loosely –

37

second. The third looked nervous, constantly scanning – save for last, but move quickly.

She shifted her weight forward, ready to descend.

Then stopped.

Something in their cautious formation, in the protective way the riflewoman positioned herself near the limping man, snagged at a memory she'd spent years trying to bury. Her mind unwillingly plunged back to that winter three years ago, when she'd walked a darker path alongside someone who'd taught her both survival and its steep cost.

The warehouse had once stored furniture, but now housed twelve survivors – if that word applied to the desperate collection of gaunt-faced individuals huddled around oil drum fires. She had joined them a few weeks prior, after they'd found her half-frozen in an abandoned gas station. Their leader, a rail-thin man with nicotine-stained fingers, had assessed her with calculating eyes before nodding her in.

"Another mouth to feed," he'd muttered, "but you look useful enough."

That first night, she'd met Vera Kane. Everyone called her Vex, a nickname she wore with visible pride.

"You'll need a better weapon than that," Vex had said, eyeing the kitchen knife tucked in her belt. She'd offered a machete, handle first. "This'll keep you breathing longer."

Vex stood out from the others – not just for the jagged scar running from her left temple to jaw, but for her ruthless competence. Five foot eight of controlled danger with dark hair chopped unevenly at the shoulders. Unlike the others who seemed beaten down by the world's collapse, Vex moved with deliberate purpose, as though the apocalypse had merely cleared away inconvenient social barriers.

"We're going out tomorrow," Vex told her. "Supply run. You're with me."

The next morning, they'd moved through the ruins of suburbia, checking houses methodically. Vex demonstrated efficient search patterns, pointing out overlooked storage spaces and teaching her to listen for the distinctive shuffling of the reanimated dead.

"Most survivors get themselves killed," Vex explained, prying open a cabinet with a crowbar, "because they panic. Fear is useless. So is hope. All that matters is the next step, the next meal, the next kill."

She had nodded, absorbing the lesson while scanning windows for movement.

"And the living," Vex continued, voice dropping, "they're the real threat. The infected, the dead – they're predictable. People aren't."

Four houses yielded little: some canned vegetables, batteries, half a bottle of antibiotics. The fifth house changed everything.

They heard voices from two blocks away – careless laughter, a male voice raised in argument. Vex's expression hardened as she signaled a detour toward the sound.

"What are we doing?" she whispered.

Vex's gray eyes narrowed. "Finding better supplies."

The family – father, mother, teenage son – had established themselves in a colonial-style home fortified with lumber and corrugated metal. They had a garden in the backyard, solar panels on the roof. Vex watched them through binoculars for twenty minutes, noting entry points and routines.

"They've got medicine, ammunition, probably fuel," Vex murmured. "Enough to share."

"You mean steal."

Vex turned, studying her face. "Is there a difference anymore? They have excess. We need it. Nature sorts these things out."

"We don't know they have excess."

"Nobody has three working solar panels without having other resources." Vex handed her the binoculars. "Look at their clothes – clean, intact. Look at their faces – full. While Hector back at camp is coughing blood because we have no antibiotics."

She hesitated, then took the binoculars.

"We'll wait until dark," Vex decided. "Simple in-and-out. No one gets hurt if they don't resist."

But she had seen the rifle the father carried, had watched the careful way the mother checked sightlines whenever she stepped outside. These people would resist.

Darkness fell. They waited until the lights went out in all but one room. Vex produced a small glass bottle from her pack.

"Cocktail time," she whispered, stuffing a rag into the gasoline-filled bottle. "Throw it at the opposite side of the house from where we'll enter. When they rush to deal with it, we slip in, take what we need, vanish."

The plan worked with terrifying precision. The molotov cocktail shattered against the side wall, flames spreading quickly across the dry wooden siding. Shouts erupted inside. The family emerged through the front door, the father organizing a bucket chain from their rainwater collection system.

She followed Vex through a back window, into a kitchen stocked with preserved foods. Vex pointed her toward cabinets while she headed for what appeared to be a bedroom. Two minutes later, her backpack bulged with canned goods and medications.

The mother returned unexpectedly, perhaps for more buckets. She froze at the kitchen threshold, eyes widening at the intruder. No words came – just a mother's protective fury as she rushed forward with a garden trowel clutched like a dagger.

Training took over. The machete Vex had given her swept outward in a defensive arc. Too close, too fast. Metal bit into flesh. The woman collapsed, crimson spreading across her shirt.

Horror paralyzed her as the dying woman clutched at the wound, trying to hold together what couldn't be fixed. Vex appeared in the doorway, took in the scene with a quick glance.

"Grab the food," Vex ordered, kneeling to search the dying woman's pockets, removing a ring of keys. "Happens in war. Move."

Outside, the fire had spread. The father's desperate shouts for his wife cut through the crackling flames. Vex led her through shadow-paths between houses until the sounds faded, replaced by the dull thudding of her own heartbeat in her ears.

Back at the warehouse, Vex divided their spoils, presenting antibiotics to Hector, chocolate bars to wide-eyed children. Their grateful faces blurred through her unshed tears. That night, she scrubbed blood from beneath her fingernails until the skin cracked.

Vex found her later, sitting alone in the storage mezzanine.

"First human?" Vex asked, settling beside her.

She nodded, unable to speak.

"It fractures something in you," Vex acknowledged, surprising her with the gentleness in her voice. "But that family had choices. Fortify differently. Set watches. Share with others to build community. Their insulation was their weakness."

"She was protecting her home."

"And you were protecting our people. No difference." Vex's hand tentatively covered hers, warm and steady. "This world doesn't allow for hesitation anymore. You act or you die. You did what was necessary."

The contact lingered longer than needed, Vex's thumb tracing small circles on her wrist. When their eyes met, something unspoken passed between them – recognition, perhaps, of how few connections remained in this broken world, and how desperately they clung to those that formed.

She withdrew her hand first.

Over subsequent weeks, she became Vex's shadow, learning the brutal calculus of post-collapse survival. Vex proved a demanding but thorough teacher – demonstrating how to create distractions to navigate infected-heavy areas, how to quickly assess which buildings merited the risk of exploration, how to set snares for small game.

"Always preserve ammunition," Vex instructed, dispatching a reanimated corpse with her hunting knife. "Sound attracts more problems than it solves."

They made an efficient team. She handled the methodical aspects – finding safe paths, securing perimeters, maintaining equipment – while Vex navigated the human element, deciding which survivors to avoid, which to approach, which to target.

Increasingly, it was the latter. What began as occasional necessity devolved into Vex's preferred methodology: locate survivors with resources, observe their patterns, exploit weaknesses, take what they needed. Sometimes at night, sometimes through deception, sometimes through force.

She told herself each raid was justified. The medicine saved Hector and two children with respiratory infections. The ammunition protected them from a gang that tried to seize the warehouse. The food carried them through three weeks when game grew scarce.

But justifications wore thinner with each successful operation. Vex grew bolder, taking more than immediate necessities. Watches. Books. Alcohol. Small luxuries that couldn't be prioritized in a world of essential survival.

"We deserve some comforts," Vex argued when questioned. "We're the ones with the courage to take action. The strong survive by making difficult choices."

One evening, Vex returned to their shared corner of the warehouse with a bottle of scotch salvaged from some forgotten liquor cabinet. They passed it between them as Vex recounted stories from before – a life of perpetual motion, never settling, always testing boundaries.

"I was never built for their world," Vex confessed, words slightly slurred. "All those arbitrary rules about property and politeness. This world makes more sense. Direct action, direct consequences."

The alcohol warmed her chest as Vex edged closer, their shoulders touching.

"We're the same, you and I," Vex murmured. "You try to hide it, but I see how you calculate every move, weigh every risk. You were made for this time."

"I'm not like you."

"No?" Vex's fingers brushed hair from her face, lingering at her temple. "You adapt. You survive. You do what's necessary without flinching. That's why we work so well together. That's why I—"

Vex stopped, gray eyes searching hers in the dim light. The unfinished sentiment hung between them. For a moment, she glimpsed something vulnerable beneath Vex's hardened exterior – a longing for connection beyond tactical alliance.

She looked away first, unable to face what Vex offered – not just companionship, but validation of the darkness growing inside her.

Spring brought new tensions. Food stores dwindled as more survivors joined their group, drawn by rumors of relative safety. The warehouse leader grew increasingly dependent on Vex's ability to "acquire" necessities. With each successful raid, Vex's influence expanded, her methods less questioned.

Then came the hospital expedition.

"Military tried to establish a treatment center there," Vex explained, spreading hand-drawn maps before their now-expanded team of six. "Abandoned during evacuation, but they left supplies behind. Locked down tight in the pharmacy section."

"Infected inside?" asked Mateo, a former construction worker who'd joined them a month prior.

"Definitely," Vex nodded. "But mostly contained to the lower floors. We enter through the roof access, work our way down to the fourth floor pharmacy."

The plan seemed reasonable until Vex revealed the final element: "We'll need a diversion to draw the infected away from the main stairwell when we exit. Fire should work."

"A fire in a hospital filled with infected?" she questioned. "We'd be starting an inferno."

Vex shrugged. "Buildings burn all the time now. Makes no difference."

"What if there are other survivors using the building for shelter?"

"Then they should have secured the pharmacy before we did." Vex's tone ended further discussion.

The mission proceeded the following morning. Their team of six moved through suburbs toward the community hospital, a six-story building standing relatively intact against the skyline.

Two team members fell during the approach – one to a fast-moving infected that burst from a garden shed, another to a simple misstep that sent him tumbling through rotted floorboards, his scream cut short by a broken neck.

Four remained. They accessed the roof through an adjacent building, crossed an improvised bridge of wooden planks spanning the alley, and entered through a maintenance door. The hospital's interior reeked of decay and antiseptic chemicals, an incongruous combination that burned the sinuses.

Navigating dark corridors by flashlight, they encountered scattered infected – hospital staff in bloodied scrubs, patients in tattered gowns. They eliminated threats silently with blades and crossbow bolts, preserving ammunition and maintaining stealth.

The pharmacy's reinforced door required the crowbar, the noise of metal against metal setting her teeth on edge. Inside, they found what Vex had promised: antibiotics, painkillers, surgical supplies, even vaccines requiring no refrigeration. They filled backpacks methodically, marking a significant victory against the constant threat of mundane infections that now regularly claimed lives.

"Set the charges," Vex ordered Mateo, who began placing homemade incendiary devices near oxygen tanks at the nursing station.

"This is excessive," she argued, keeping her voice low. "We have what we came for. Let's leave quietly."

"We need clear exit paths," Vex countered. "This ensures nothing follows us home."

"It's unnecessary risk."

"It's necessary protection." Vex's expression hardened. "Don't get squeamish now."

As Mateo worked, they heard it – voices, unmistakably human, a floor below. Not the guttural moans of infected, but clear communication. Other survivors.

She caught Vex's eye. "We need to warn them about the fire."

"We need to stick to the plan."

"They'll be trapped."

"Not our problem."

A line crystallized between them – moral boundary rendered in perfect clarity. The machete at her hip suddenly felt heavier, the blood of the mother from months ago fresher in memory.

"I'm going to warn them," she decided, moving toward the stairwell.

Vex's hand clamped around her arm. "You compromise this operation, you compromise all of us."

She pulled free. "There are children's voices down there."

Something shifted in Vex's expression – calculation replacing anger. "Fine. Tell Mateo to finish up while we check it out."

They descended together to the third floor, following the sounds to a former maternity ward converted to living quarters. Through cloudy window panels, they observed approximately twenty survivors – families with children, elderly, a community that had established some semblance of normalcy within the hospital's walls.

"They've been here all along," she whispered. "We need to call off the fire."

Vex studied the scene, eyes narrowing. "Look at their supplies. Organized. Clean clothing. They've been hoarding."

"They've been surviving, same as us."

"With medicines we need, while our people get infections from minor cuts." Vex unholstered her pistol. "Change of plans. We're taking everything."

"No." Her hand moved to the machete. "These aren't isolated homesteaders. This is a community with children."

"Children who'll have better chances with us," Vex argued. "We have the numbers, the warehouse. They have medicines we need."

"We already have medicines. We just raided the pharmacy."

"Not enough. Never enough." Vex's voice took on an edge she'd never heard before. "You've gone soft. All this time, I thought you understood what it takes."

"I understand you're willing to burn children alive for antibiotics we already have."

Vex's laugh held no humor. "You think that's where I draw the line? After everything we've done?" She stepped closer. "I've seen you cut down people for less. You're just like me. Stop pretending otherwise."

The accusation struck with physical force. Not because it was false, but because of how closely it approximated truth.

Every raid, every theft, every justification had drawn her closer to becoming what Vex already was – someone who saw other humans as merely resources or obstacles.

An explosion rocked the building – Mateo had triggered the devices early.

Vex recovered first, raising her weapon toward the maternity ward doors. "Opportunity presents itself. When they rush out confused, we take control."

"No." She drew the machete.

Vex's eyes widened slightly, then narrowed. "You would choose strangers over your own people? Over me?"

The question carried weight beyond tactical disagreement. In Vex's expression, she read not just anger, but betrayal of a deeper nature – rejection not just of her plan, but of her worldview, her offered connection.

"I'm choosing to stop this before we lose whatever's left of our humanity."

Smoke filled the corridor. Shouts of alarm emerged from the ward as its occupants mobilized. Vex repositioned, taking aim at the doors.

She moved without hesitation, machete sweeping in a controlled arc toward Vex's wrist. Blade met flesh. The gun clattered to floor tiles as Vex howled in pain and rage.

What followed was chaos – alarms sounding, sprinklers activating, infected drawn by noise converging from lower floors. The ward doors burst open, survivors emerging with makeshift weapons, fighting through confusion.

Vex clutched her bleeding wrist, eyes burning with betrayal. "You've killed us all."

"I've stopped you from killing innocent people."

"There are no innocent people anymore." Vex backed away as approaching infected rounded the corner. "There's just us and them. And you've chosen your side."

She never saw Vex kick the emergency exit door closed between them, separating her from their planned escape route. The clang of metal echoed with finality as infected closed in from both directions.

Survival instinct took over. She fought through creatures that had once been patients and staff, machete carving red arcs through the air. The survivors from the ward battled alongside her, not questioning her presence, focused only on the immediate threat.

Hours later, when the infected had been cleared and the fires contained, she collapsed against a wall, exhausted beyond measure. A young doctor treated her wounds and offered water.

"You tried to warn us," the doctor said. Not a question.

She nodded.

"The others with you?"

"Not with me anymore."

The doctor seemed to understand what remained unspoken. "You're welcome to stay. We can use someone with your skills."

But she knew Vex would return – with more people, better prepared, driven by vengeance and practicality in equal measure. Her presence endangered these people who had preserved something she had nearly lost.

She left before dawn, carrying only her weapons and minimal supplies. At the hospital edge, she found Mateo's body, throat torn open by infected teeth. Of Vex, there was no sign – only a blood trail leading away from the building, testimony to survival despite injury.

In the months that followed, she avoided other survivors, keeping to rural areas, hunting small game, scavenging abandoned properties that others overlooked. Sometimes she caught rumors of a group led by a woman with a distinctive facial scar and missing hand, known for ruthless efficiency in claiming territory.

She moved in opposite directions, carrying the weight of what she'd almost become.

The words she'd spoken in that hospital corridor were the last she'd offer freely to strangers. Every syllable uttered was a connection formed, a vulnerability exposed. Vex had shown her how words could manipulate, could justify horrors, could twist morality until black seemed white. The fewer words exchanged, the fewer lies told – to others or to herself.

Silence became her armor, protecting whatever remained of the person she'd been before. She communicated through gesture, through action, through the decisive swing of a blade or the precise aim of her shotgun. The essentials required no discussion.

Lone travelers lived longer anyway. No arguments about direction, no debates about resources, no betrayals when priorities shifted. In solitude, she found clarity – each decision hers alone, each consequence accepted without complaint.

The only voice she heard now was her own, echoing in her mind, weighing options, calculating risks. Sometimes, in dreams, she heard Vex's voice too – that final accusation. "You're just like me." The fear that this might still be true kept her moving, kept her separate, kept her silent.

Now, crouched above the three travelers on the road below, she recognized the precipice. Hunger gnawed at her stomach. The logical calculation of risk versus reward balanced heavily toward attack.

Vex would not have hesitated.

She secured the machete in its sheath and backed away from the ridge. The travelers continued their journey, unaware of how close they had come to ambush, unaware of the ghost that watched them pass.

Some lines, once seen, could not be uncrossed.

She would find another way to survive. She always did.

Ed Rodriguez

No Horizon: Blood Trail

The mistake happened during the simplest of tasks.

She was sharpening the machete against a whetstone, her back against the wall of an abandoned mechanic's garage, when the blade slipped. The cut across her left palm was deep, severing through skin and fat to the connective tissue beneath. Blood welled immediately, running down her wrist in thick rivulets.

For five seconds, she simply observed the wound with clinical detachment. No tendons severed. No arterial spray. Painful, but not immediately life-threatening.

She set the machete aside and retrieved her first aid kit from her pack. The garage had been secure for two nights—heavy metal door barricaded, windows already boarded by

59

previous occupants, a small access hatch to the roof for emergency escape. She had time to treat this properly.

Working methodically, she irrigated the wound with purified water from her canteen, flushing out metal particles from the blade. Using her free hand and her teeth, she tore open an alcohol wipe, hissing silently as she cleaned the laceration. The antiseptic burn was familiar—a small price for preventing infection.

The wound needed stitches. She threaded a curved suture needle, gripping it with improvised forceps fashioned from a multi-tool. The first puncture through her skin sent a fresh wave of pain radiating up her arm. She ignored it, focusing instead on the mechanics of the procedure—small, even stitches, each tied off individually in case one should fail.

A memory flashed unbidden as she worked: gentle hands guiding hers, a calm voice explaining the importance of tension in each suture. "Too tight constricts blood flow. Too loose won't hold." The voice, almost forgotten now, belonged to someone who had once mattered. Someone who had ensured she would survive long after they were gone. She pushed the memory away, but the phantom touch lingered on her fingers.

Seven stitches later, she covered the wound with a thin layer of antibiotic ointment, then wrapped it in gauze. The dressing would need changing daily. The stitches would limit her left hand's dexterity for at least a week. An inconvenience in a world where inconveniences killed.

She cleaned her tools and the blood from the concrete floor, leaving no trace of injury that might attract scavengers or the infected, whose sense of smell seemed heightened by the disease. As she worked, she mentally adjusted her plans, calculating new risks and limitations.

The machete was her primary close-quarters weapon. The handaxe would have to serve instead, requiring her to get closer to threats. Her ability to climb would be compromised. The shotgun would be more difficult to pump one-handed. Every aspect of survival had just become more complicated.

A dull ache settled in her chest, distinct from the throbbing in her hand. It was the weight of solitude, heavier in moments of vulnerability. She allowed herself three seconds to acknowledge it before forcing it down, back into the compartment where she kept all things that served no survival purpose.

Outside, the afternoon sun cast long shadows across the junked cars surrounding the garage. She needed to hunt before dark, injured or not. Her supplies were dangerously low.

She slung the shotgun across her back, positioned the handaxe at her belt within easy reach of her right hand, and tucked the survival knife into her boot. The crowbar went through a loop on her pack. Her gear minimal but complete, she slipped out through the roof access, scanning the surroundings before descending to ground level.

The small town had been picked clean months ago, but the surrounding woodland still offered potential game. She moved through the overgrown streets with practiced silence, her footfalls deliberately placed to avoid disturbing the gravel and broken glass that littered the cracked asphalt.

A movement in her peripheral vision brought her to an immediate halt. Two hundred yards ahead, a lone infected wandered aimlessly between abandoned storefronts. Its jerky gait and disoriented movements suggested late-stage infection— dangerous but predictable. She changed course, giving it a wide berth.

The forest edge behind the town's old elementary school

offered natural concealment. She entered the treeline cautiously, alert for signs of human or infected presence. Finding none, she advanced deeper into the woods.

After twenty minutes, she discovered what she sought—fresh deer tracks pressed into the soft earth near a small stream. She knelt, careful not to put pressure on her injured hand, and examined the impressions. Small deer, probably malnourished like everything else in this broken ecosystem, but meat nonetheless.

The stream gurgled softly, momentarily bringing back the sound of a child's laughter. For an instant, her chest constricted with an emotion she refused to name. Had there once been fishing trips here? Family picnics along these banks? She pushed away the thoughts. The past was a luxury she couldn't afford.

She followed the tracks upstream, moving slowly and testing each step to avoid alerting her prey. The throbbing in her hand intensified with the exertion, but she compartmentalized the pain, focusing only on the hunt.

The doe came into view in a small clearing, head lowered to drink from the stream. She raised the shotgun, calculating the shot. At this range, the spread would ensure a clean kill without damaging too much meat. Her injured hand struggled to stabilize the weapon, trembling slightly as she aimed.

The blast echoed through the trees. The deer collapsed instantly.

She remained frozen, listening as the shotgun report reverberated and faded. Any infected within a mile would be drawn to the sound. She had minutes to harvest what she needed and retreat.

Approaching the fallen deer, she worked quickly with the survival knife, removing the most valuable cuts of meat and placing them in a plastic bag from her pack. The process was awkward with one good hand, taking twice as long as usual. Blood soaked through her bandage as she worked, the stitches straining against the repetitive movements.

A distant snarl reached her ears. They were coming.

She secured the meat in her pack and retreated toward a different section of town, unwilling to lead threats back to her shelter. The injured hand throbbed in time with her quickened pulse, warm blood trickling between her fingers as she moved.

Halfway back to town, she paused to rebandage the wound. The stitches had held, but the laceration oozed steadily.

She applied pressure, knowing that continuing blood loss, however minor, would eventually weaken her. Weakness meant death in this world.

For a moment, staring at her bloody palm, a wave of profound loneliness washed over her. Once, someone would have dressed this wound for her, would have insisted she rest while they hunted. Now there was only her own reflection in a shard of broken mirror she carried for checking around corners. She pushed the feeling away with practiced discipline, but it left a hollow space behind her ribs.

The sound of breaking branches came from behind. She turned, handaxe drawn, to face the threat.

Three infected burst from the treeline, running with that unnatural, loping gait that defied their emaciated forms. Their eyes, bloodshot and wild, fixed on her immediately. The scent of fresh blood had drawn them like sharks.

There was no outrunning them in their frenzied state. She backed against a large oak tree, limiting their angles of approach, and readied the handaxe in her right hand.

The first infected reached her with arms outstretched, yellowed nails grasping for flesh. She sidestepped, driving the

65

handaxe into the base of its skull where it met the spine. The infected dropped instantly.

But the axe stuck in bone. As she struggled to wrench it free, the second infected slammed into her, its fetid breath in her face. Its weight drove her backward against the tree, knocking the wind from her lungs. She released the embedded axe and drew her knife with her good hand, driving it upward under the infected's jaw and into its brain.

Hot blood and cerebrospinal fluid spilled over her hand as she pushed the twitching body away. The third infected was nearly upon her. No time to retrieve the knife.

She ducked under its grasping arms and delivered a powerful kick to its knee, shattering the joint with an audible crack. As it stumbled, she pulled the crowbar from her pack and swung it in a wide arc. The hooked end caught the infected in the temple, tearing away a chunk of skull and brain matter.

Silence fell over the forest once more. She retrieved her weapons, wiping them clean on the clothing of the fallen infected. Her bandage was now soaked crimson, the gauze completely saturated. Worse, her jacket sleeve was spattered with infected blood. She removed the contaminated garment immediately, stuffing it into an outer pocket of her pack for proper disposal later.

The exertion had taken its toll. Her vision swam slightly at the edges—the beginning stages of blood loss combined with adrenaline crash. She needed to treat the wound again and rest, but not here surrounded by corpses that would attract more infected.

She oriented herself and moved west, toward a small cluster of houses she'd noted but not yet explored. The nearest one with intact walls would serve as a temporary shelter until she could safely return to the garage.

The pain was a constant companion now, radiating from her palm up her forearm in hot waves. Each heartbeat sent a fresh pulse of discomfort through the laceration. She monitored her condition with the same detached analysis she applied to external threats—cataloging symptoms, assessing limitations, adjusting strategy.

A ranch-style house at the end of a cul-de-sac looked promising. The windows were intact, front door closed. No obvious signs of occupation or breach. She circled it once, checking angles and exits, before approaching the rear entrance.

The back door yielded to gentle pressure from the crowbar. She entered cautiously, knife ready in her good hand. The interior was dusty but undisturbed, the furniture still arranged as if awaiting the return of owners long dead.

She cleared each room methodically, compensating for her reduced combat effectiveness with increased caution. The house was empty of threats, though a withered corpse lay in the master bedroom, a bullet hole in its temple and a revolver still clutched in its skeletal hand. Self-termination had been common in the early days.

Her eyes lingered on the corpse longer than necessary. She wondered briefly about the moment of decision, about what final thoughts had occupied this stranger's mind. A photograph on the nightstand showed a smiling family—mother, father, two young children. All absent now. She turned the frame face-down with a deliberate motion, swallowing against the unexpected tightness in her throat.

In the bathroom, she found a medicine cabinet still stocked with basic supplies—expired analgesics, adhesive bandages, hydrogen peroxide. She ran the tap experimentally. Nothing. The municipal water system had failed years ago.

Using bottled water from her pack, she removed the soaked bandage and examined her wound. The stitches remained intact, but the edges of the laceration were angry and red. She cleaned it again with hydrogen peroxide, watching as the liquid bubbled against the damaged tissue.

Fresh gauze and tape from her own supplies secured the wound. She dry-swallowed two expired ibuprofen tablets from the cabinet, knowing they would have lost potency but might still take the edge off the pain.

In the kitchen, she found a cast iron frying pan and several cans of food still in the pantry—beans, corn, mixed vegetables. The labels had faded, but the cans remained sealed. Unexpected bounty.

She retrieved a small can opener from her pack and worked it around the top of a bean can, careful to minimize strain on her injured hand. The metal groaned as she pried it open. The contents smelled edible, if musty from age.

While the beans heated over a small, smokeless fire built in the fireplace, she carved thin strips from the deer meat and laid them across the pan. The protein would help her body heal. The smell of cooking food filled the house—a risk, but a calculated one. She had secured all entrances and kept the fire small.

The familiar ritual of cooking transported her momentarily to another time and place. Her hands remembered the motions taught by someone whose face was growing dimmer in her memory. There had been laughter once, warmth that had nothing to do with fire. The smell of herbs rather than just the metallic tang of canned goods. A child's eager questions about how to turn simple ingredients into a meal.

She blinked, and the memory dissolved like morning mist. The world had no place for such recollections now.

After eating, she rested with her back against the wall, facing the front door, shotgun across her lap. Sleep would be necessary for healing, but it would come in short bursts, her senses alert for danger even in unconsciousness—a survival adaptation honed over countless nights in hostile territory.

In the quiet darkness, with only the dying embers of the fire casting shadows across the abandoned living room, the weight of complete solitude pressed down upon her chest. She allowed herself, just for this moment of weakness brought on by injury and fatigue, to remember what it had felt like to sleep knowing someone else was keeping watch. To wake to the simple comfort of another human voice. To have someone who would notice if she didn't return.

A single tear tracked down her dusty cheek before she could marshal her discipline. She wiped it away with her good hand, leaving a smear of dirt and dried blood. Sentiment was as dangerous as infection in this world—it clouded judgment, created hesitation, fostered attachment to things that could not last. She shut her eyes, not surrendering to unconsciousness but methodically quieting her mind, extinguishing emotional responses until only strategic awareness remained.

Morning light filtered through the boarded windows, rousing her from shallow sleep. The pain in her hand had settled to a persistent throb. She checked the wound again—still inflamed but not showing signs of serious infection. The fresh bandage had spots of seepage but not the heavy bleeding of yesterday.

She ate cold beans from the can, conserving energy and avoiding another fire. The house had yielded several useful supplies, now carefully packed in her bag: a roll of duct tape, a small sewing kit, a slightly rusty multi-tool, and three more cans of food. The added weight was worth the resources.

Outside, a heavy mist clung to the ground, limiting visibility but also muffling sound. Advantageous conditions for movement if she was careful.

She slipped from the house and made her way through the fog-shrouded neighborhood, orienting herself by the position of the sun's dim glow through the haze. The mechanic's garage was nearly a mile away. Under normal circumstances, a simple journey. With her injury and limited visibility, significantly more dangerous.

The distant moan stopped her mid-stride. Somewhere ahead, hidden in the mist, walked the reanimated dead. Unlike the infected, these moved slowly, without purpose or direction—animated corpses driven by base instincts to feed. Their eyesight was poor, but their hearing remained acute.

She lowered herself to a crouch, using parked cars as cover. Through the swirling fog, dark shapes became visible—five reanimated, wandering in loose formation down the center of the street. Their flesh hung in tatters, months or years into decay. The disease preserved them beyond normal decomposition, creating a grotesque parody of life that could continue for years if the brain remained intact.

Their position blocked her most direct route back to the garage. She could wait them out, but the mist wouldn't last forever. Once visibility improved, her chances of being spotted increased dramatically.

She reached into her pack and removed an empty can from yesterday's meal. She dropped a small pebble inside, then sealed the open top with duct tape, creating a simple noisemaker.

Moving to the edge of her cover, she shook the can gently, creating a subtle rattling sound. The nearest reanimated turned toward the noise, its milky eyes scanning the fog. She tossed the can down a side street, where it clattered against the pavement.

The sound drew all five reanimated away from her path. They shambled toward the disturbance with singular focus, disappearing into the mist. She waited thirty seconds, then moved quickly across the exposed street, keeping her footfalls light despite her haste.

A few blocks later, the mechanic's garage came into view. She approached cautiously, checking for signs that her sanctuary had been discovered or breached in her absence. The barricade remained undisturbed. She slipped in through the roof access, securing it behind her.

Inside, she unpacked her new supplies and the remaining deer meat, arranging everything with methodical precision. The venison would need to be preserved. Using twine from her pack, she created a simple rack from which to hang strips of meat to dry near a small, ventilated fire.

As she worked, she assessed her condition honestly. The hand injury would limit her effectiveness for at least a week, possibly longer. Her normal scavenging range would need to be reduced. Combat would be last resort only. She would need to rely more heavily on traps and avoidance strategies until the wound healed sufficiently.

With the meat hanging to dry and her supplies organized, she allowed herself a moment of genuine rest. She removed her boots, checked them for damage, then stretched out on her sleeping bag, eyes closed but senses alert. The pain in her hand had become a constant companion, neither intensifying nor abating, simply existing as another fact of her narrowed world.

A surge of self-directed anger flared unexpectedly. The injury had made her weak—not just physically but mentally. She'd allowed memories to surface, emotions to breach her carefully constructed walls. Sentimentality was a luxury that killed in this world. It dulled reflexes, clouded judgment, created hesitation when only decisive action meant survival.

She clenched her jaw, disgusted by her lapse. The person who had taught her medical skills—those gentle hands guiding her through sutures and wound care—belonged to the past. So too did the one who'd shown her how to hunt silently and survive in this broken world. Both would be disappointed by such weakness. The lessons hadn't just been about skills but about hardening oneself against the past, against connection, against anything that might compromise the cold calculation necessary to endure.

Tomorrow would bring new challenges. She would face them with renewed detachment—the calculating pragmatism and grim determination that had kept her alive while billions died. The injury was merely another obstacle to overcome, another problem to solve in a world defined by problems without solutions. She would be harder. Colder. It was the only way.

She drifted into guarded sleep, one hand on the shotgun beside her, the other curled protectively against her chest. Outside, the mist began to lift, revealing the ruins of civilization to the indifferent sun above. Another day of survival in a world

Ed Rodriguez

where surviving was the only victory left.

No Horizon: Cold Wind Blows

The sound of her boots crunching through the half-frozen slush echoed too loudly in the abandoned suburban street. She paused, listening for any response to the noise. Nothing immediate, but her eyes narrowed at a thin trail of smoke rising from a chimney three blocks ahead. Someone was burning something. Careless. Desperate. Or a trap.

She adjusted the worn leather straps of her backpack, feeling the reassuring weight of her supplies. The pump-action shotgun rested across her back, secured but accessible in one fluid motion if needed. The machete hung at her left hip, opposite the survival knife on her right thigh. The crowbar was slotted through a loop on her pack, and the hand axe was tucked into her belt at the small of her back.

Five houses to check before nightfall. Five potential sources of supplies. Five potential death traps.

The temperature was dropping. Her breath formed crystalline clouds in the air as she moved forward, staying close to the abandoned vehicles and overgrown hedges. The snow had started two days ago, and the world had transformed into something even more hostile than before. The infected moved slower in the cold—a small advantage—but so did she. And the dead ones, the truly dead ones that still walked, they didn't seem to notice the cold at all.

She approached the first house systematically, circling it completely before even considering entry. The snow around it was disturbed—tracks leading to and from the back door, some fresh, some partially filled with new snow. Two sets, maybe three. Too risky. She marked an X on the mailbox with a piece of chalk and moved on. A signal to herself: not worth it.

The second house showed no tracks, but a window on the second floor had been smashed inward. Birds maybe, or someone who had come and gone weeks ago. Still, she watched the house for fifteen minutes from behind the rusted shell of a minivan, noting any movement, any sound.

When she finally approached, it was from the rear, through a wooden gate hanging half off its hinges. The kitchen door was locked, but the crowbar made short work of that. She paused after the crack of splintering wood, waiting again, listening. The crowbar remained in her hand, a familiar weight, ready to swing at the first sign of movement.

Inside, the kitchen had been thoroughly ransacked, cabinets hanging open, drawers pulled out. She moved efficiently, checking corners, closets, under furniture. The house groaned and settled in the cold, but nothing moved. Upstairs first, then down to the basement—standard procedure. Never leave something above you unchecked.

The upstairs bathroom yielded half a bottle of hydrogen peroxide and a still-sealed package of dental floss. Both went into her pack. The bedrooms were empty except for a child's room where she found a magnifying glass still in its packaging. Fire starter. Useful.

In the child's room, her eyes lingered momentarily on a small stuffed rabbit, dirty but intact, propped against a pillow. For a second—just one—her fingers twitched toward it. Then her hand fell back to her side. Useless weight. No practical purpose.

She moved on.

The pantry in the kitchen had been cleaned out, but she knelt down, running her fingers along the edges of the linoleum. One corner peeled up slightly. She worked the knife under it and pulled back a section to reveal a small cache: three cans of vegetables, a can of spam, and a bottle of multivitamins. Someone's emergency stock, forgotten in their rush to evacuate, or hidden from others in the house. She packed it all, leaving nothing behind.

In the basement, she found an old workbench with a few forgotten tools. A new roll of duct tape went into the pack. Duct tape was worth its weight in gold. A package of batteries were tested against her tongue—still some charge. They joined the other supplies.

She was closing the pack when she heard it. A wet, gasping breath from the corner of the basement. Her shotgun was up and aimed before her eyes fully adjusted to the darkness of the corner.

It was an infected—fresh, still in the early stages. It had been a middle-aged man, now gaunt, eyes bloodshot and skin slicked with sweat despite the cold. A house resident who'd hidden away after infection, perhaps, or someone who'd broken in and succumbed down here. It was chained to a support beam, hands cuffed behind its back. Its eyes were wild, mouth frothing as it thrashed against the restraints at the sight of her.

Someone had left it here. Recently.

She assessed the situation with clinical detachment. The chain would hold for now, but it was attached to a wooden beam. Given enough time and frenzy, the infected might break free. The noise it was making could attract others. The shotgun would be too loud.

She set her pack down and drew the machete, approaching from an angle the infected couldn't reach if the chain broke. One clean stroke separated its head from its body, the spray of infected blood splattering across the concrete floor. She stepped back, avoiding the spray. The body thrashed for a few more seconds, then went still, though the head continued to gnash its teeth, eyes blinking in rage.

That's when she heard the footsteps above. Multiple sets. Heavy. Deliberate.

Raiders. Coming to check their trapped pet.

She was up the basement stairs in seconds, keeping low,

machete still in hand, listening. Three voices, two male, one female. They were in the kitchen now, discussing the broken door. They hadn't heard her over their own noise. Careless.

"Check the basement," one said. "I'll take upstairs."

No time to set a proper ambush. She pressed herself against the wall beside the basement door, calculating angles, timing. The door opened inward. The machete would be too unwieldy in the tight space.

She drew the survival knife instead and waited. When the woman stepped through, she drove the knife up under her jaw, clamping her other hand over her mouth to muffle the sound. The woman went down heavily, and she lowered her to the floor as quietly as possible, retrieving her knife.

One down. The element of surprise was gone now. She heard the creak of floorboards above—the second raider was already upstairs. The third was moving through the living room, calling out to his friend in a harsh whisper.

She moved to the kitchen doorway, evaluating options. The living room raider would find his dead friend any moment. The shotgun would alert the one upstairs and potentially draw more danger from outside. She needed something else.

Her eyes settled on the crowbar, still resting on the counter where she'd left it. She grabbed it and moved towards the living room. The third raider was bent over his friend's body, shaking her, not yet comprehending what had happened.

She crossed the room in three silent strides and brought the crowbar down on the back of his skull with a dull crack. He collapsed forward onto his friend. The crowbar was more efficient than she'd expected—cleaner than the knife, less messy than the machete.

Two down. One to go.

The floorboards creaked again overhead. She had time now. Retrieving her pack and shotgun from the basement, she moved to the base of the stairs and waited, crowbar in one hand, knife in the other.

The last raider called down to his friends. No answer. He called again, suspicion in his voice. The stairs creaked as he began his descent. She remained perfectly still, controlling her breathing, calculating the exact moment to strike.

He was faster than expected, and more cautious. He came down with a gun drawn—a small revolver. She pivoted out from her position as he reached the third step from the bottom, slashing at his gun hand with the knife. He fired reflexively, the bullet embedding in the wall behind her. The knife found its mark, slicing across his fingers, and the gun clattered to the floor.

He lunged at her with his other hand, revealing a hunting knife. She deflected with the crowbar, but he was strong, pushing her back against the wall. The hunting knife inched closer to her throat as they grappled.

She drove her knee up, connecting with his groin. His grip loosened just enough. She twisted the crowbar, hooking the curved end behind his knife arm and yanking down sharply. Something in his elbow popped. He howled. The hunting knife fell.

Three rapid strikes with the crowbar—temple, throat, temple. He crumpled to the floor.

Three down.

She checked each body methodically, gathering ammunition, a bottle of antibiotics, beef jerky, a lighter with fuel, and a compass. The gun was a .38 Special with three rounds remaining. Not her preferred weapon, but it could be useful as a last resort. It went into her pack.

Something caught her eye as she searched the last raider

—a worn photograph tucked inside his jacket. She pulled it out: two children and a woman, all smiling, standing in front of a cabin. On the back, written in faded ink: "Come home safe."

Her jaw tightened almost imperceptibly. She slipped the photo back into the man's jacket, positioning it exactly as she'd found it. These men had chained an infected human being in a basement as bait. Whatever life they'd had before, whatever waited for them somewhere, didn't matter now.

A quick check of the rest of the house confirmed no immediate threats. The encounter had taken less than five minutes from start to finish, but the gunshot complicated things. She needed to move on immediately.

Outside, the light was starting to fade. Snow was falling again, harder now, which would cover her tracks but also make travel more difficult. She scanned the street, identifying movement two houses down. The shambling gait was unmistakable—reanimated dead, drawn by the gunshot. Two of them, moving slowly through the accumulating snow.

She could avoid them easily by going around the back of the houses, but checked her position relative to the smoke she'd seen earlier. The chimney house was directly past the walking dead. Going around would waste daylight she couldn't afford to lose.

Eliminating them would be simple. The shotgun was too loud. She opted for the hand axe, moving towards them with purposeful strides through the deepening snow.

The walking dead turned towards her as she approached, jaws working mechanically, arms outstretched. The first one had been an elderly woman, now a gray-skinned husk with milky eyes and half its scalp torn away. The second had been younger, male, its throat torn out but its body otherwise intact.

She dispatched them with mechanical efficiency—one axe blow to each skull, aiming for the temple where the bone was thinnest. The axe blade sank into the decayed flesh with a sound like an axe hitting a ripe watermelon. No blood splatter from these ones; they'd been dead too long for that. They collapsed like puppets with cut strings.

She wiped the axe blade clean on the tattered clothing of one corpse and continued down the street.

The house with the chimney smoke required more care. As she drew closer, she could see it was better fortified than the others—boards over windows, a makeshift barrier of furniture blocking the front yard. Someone was established here, which meant they might have supplies worth taking, but also meant they'd be more prepared to defend them.

She observed the house from the shelter of a large oak tree in a neighboring yard. One entrance visible—the front door, barricaded but with a system of ropes that could be used to open it from inside. Two people had exited and returned in the time she watched—a man in his fifties and a younger woman, possibly his daughter. They'd gone to a shed in the back with empty containers and returned with them full. Water collection system, probably.

The smoke suggested a wood stove or fireplace. Risky in the apocalypse, but necessary in this cold. They were surviving, but their security was flawed. Too much focus on the front entrance. The second-floor windows were boarded, but one board was loose, moving slightly in the wind.

She could take what they had. It would be easy enough. Wait until dark, use the tree branches to reach the loose board, slip in while they slept. People in established locations kept the best supplies.

As she considered her approach, a child's face appeared

briefly at an unboarded portion of a first-floor window—a girl, no more than six or seven. The child was painfully thin, her collarbones visible even from this distance. Behind her, the flutter of movement revealed a second child, smaller, clutching what looked like a doll made from rags and twine.

Something shifted behind her ribs, a dull ache she hadn't felt in a long time. Hunger was familiar to her—a constant companion in this world—but the hollow look in the child's eyes stirred something she'd methodically buried beneath layers of survival instinct.

The man and woman emerged again, carrying what appeared to be a single, small rabbit. Tonight's meal for four, then. Not nearly enough.

She remained motionless, calculating. The family clearly had a water system and heat but was running dangerously low on food. Taking their supplies would doom them. The children wouldn't survive a week.

Unbidden, her mind returned to the stuffed rabbit in the abandoned house, the photograph in the raider's pocket. Fragments of a world long dead. Useless sentimentality that got people killed.

And yet.

She retreated silently, circling back to one of the houses she'd already cleared. From her pack, she removed two cans of vegetables and the spam. A measured decision: she could replace these items. The family might not find food before the children weakened beyond recovery.

Approaching the fortified house from behind, she located their water collection system—a series of tarps feeding into rain barrels. Efficient design. Near it was a small woodpile covered with plastic sheeting, newly chopped logs stacked neatly. She placed the cans on the woodpile where they would be discovered during the next trip for firewood.

The snow crunched behind her.

Her hand was already moving to her knife when the shovel struck her shoulder. Not a killing blow—the man had hesitated. A mistake. She rolled with the impact, absorbing most of the force, and came up in a defensive crouch.

The father stood ten feet away, shovel gripped in white-knuckled hands, eyes wild with desperate protectiveness. Not a raider—just a man defending his family from a perceived threat.

"Get away from my house!" His voice cracked, hoarse

from disuse or fear.

She held her hands away from her weapons, palms open, eyes never leaving his. The cans lay visible on the woodpile between them. His gaze flicked to them, then back to her, confusion now mixing with the fear.

She took one step backward. A gesture of de-escalation.

He hesitated, glancing at the cans again. Understanding dawned in his eyes, followed immediately by suspicion. "What kind of trick is this?"

She took another step back. Another.

He lurched forward suddenly, swinging the shovel in a wide arc. "It's poison, isn't it? You think I'm stupid?"

She sidestepped easily, but the accusation struck deeper than the shovel could have. Of course he would think that. Trust was extinct.

"We've seen your kind before," he spat, advancing again. "Taking what's not yours. Watching us. Planning."

She continued backing away, hands still open, making no move toward her weapons. The shovel whistled through the air again, closer this time.

"Dad?" The child's voice from the doorway of the house

froze them both. The girl she'd seen earlier stood there, the smaller child behind her.

The man's attention wavered for just one second. She could have drawn her knife, disabled him, been gone before he hit the ground.

But the children were watching.

"Get back inside!" the man shouted, panic edging his voice.

The distraction cost him. His foot slipped on the icy ground, and he stumbled forward, the shovel's momentum carrying him closer than he'd intended. Too close.

Instinct took over. She twisted, caught his wrist, and used his forward momentum to drive him hard into the ground. The air left his lungs in a painful whoosh. The shovel clattered away.

She could hear the children screaming now. The younger woman appeared in the doorway, a kitchen knife in her hand, face a mask of terror.

The man thrashed beneath her grip, desperate but untrained. She could end this in seconds. Clean. Efficient.

The children's cries cut through her calculations.

Decision made, she wrenched the man's arm up behind his

back—enough force to dislocate his shoulder with a sickening pop. He screamed. A non-lethal injury. Painful, debilitating, but survivable.

She released him and backed away, keeping her eye on the younger woman who was now rushing forward with the knife.

"Take the food," she said, her voice barely above a whisper, pointing to the cans. Her first and only words to them. "He needs medical attention."

The father writhed on the ground, clutching his useless arm, face contorted in agony. The young woman hesitated, torn between attacking and tending to him.

She used the moment to disappear into the gathering darkness, the sounds of the children's crying fading behind her.

A catastrophic error in judgment. She'd allowed sentiment to override strategy. The moment she'd placed those cans down, she'd created vulnerability—not just for herself, but ironically for the very family she'd tried to help. Now a man was injured, children traumatized, a young woman left to care for them all with one less able body.

Her shoulder throbbed where the shovel had struck.

92

Nothing broken, but it would bruise badly. A physical reminder of the cost of misplaced compassion.

As she moved away from the house, her shoulders felt heavier, burdened not by the loss of supplies but by the confirmation of what she'd always known: kindness was a liability in this world. Community was a construct of the past. Those who survived alone, survived longest.

The last light was fading fast as she reached her target destination—a small water treatment substation at the edge of the suburb. Concrete walls, metal door, minimal windows, all set slightly below ground level. Defensible. Insulated. Overlooked by most survivors because it appeared to have no practical resources.

She'd marked it two weeks ago while passing through. Now, she returned to claim it as a temporary shelter from the storm.

The padlock on the door was still intact. Good sign. She broke it with targeted strikes from the hand axe—three precise hits that minimized noise. Inside, the small facility was untouched. A desk, some filing cabinets, a small employee restroom. Most importantly, a maintenance room with a cot for workers on overnight shifts.

She secured the door behind her using wire from her pack threaded through the interior handle and attached to an empty filing cabinet. Anyone trying to enter would knock over the cabinet, creating noise. Simple but effective.

The concrete walls would hold in any heat she generated and block the howling wind outside. The building was small enough to warm with minimal effort. She retrieved a small alcohol stove from her pack and started heating one of her remaining cans of vegetables.

As the small flame worked, she meticulously cleaned each of her weapons. Blood and tissue left on blades led to contamination and disease. The survival knife, machete, hand axe, and crowbar were all wiped down, edges checked for nicks or damage. The shotgun was inspected, though it hadn't been fired. Seventeen shells remained. The newly acquired revolver was cleaned and loaded fully with the additional bullets.

She ate methodically, focusing on the nutrition rather than the taste. A multivitamin washed down with a carefully measured amount of water. Calories and nutrients to replace what she'd burned. Less than usual tonight, but sufficient.

The wind howled outside as the snowstorm intensified, rattling the small windows of the facility. She allowed herself a small measure of satisfaction. The insulated concrete structure, overlooked by others, was now fifteen degrees warmer than the outside air and would maintain that difference through the night. Her body heat under the emergency blanket would be sufficient. No fire needed, no smoke to give away her position.

She arranged her pack to serve as a pillow, weapons laid out in order of reach priority—knife, revolver, shotgun. Sleep would come in measured increments. Three hours, check surroundings. Three more hours, check again. Before dawn, move on.

As she closed her eyes for the first sleep cycle, an image returned unbidden—the small girl at the door, the horror in her eyes as she watched her father fall. The screams. The fear. The unmistakable hatred.

She had tried to help and instead had become exactly what the man accused her of being: a threat. The food she'd left might feed them tonight, but at what cost? A father with a dislocated shoulder couldn't chop wood, couldn't hunt, couldn't protect. She'd made their situation worse, not better.

The calculation had been flawed from the start. Sentiment was a defect in reasoning, a malfunction in the survival algorithm. The weak helped the weak and both perished together. The strong survived alone. Nature's law still governed this broken world, perhaps more purely than before.

Her shoulder throbbed where the shovel had struck—a physical reminder of the lesson. She would carry the bruise for days, a memento of naive miscalculation. It would fade, but the reinforced knowledge would remain: compassion was a luxury of the old world. In this one, it was a potentially fatal error.

Tomorrow would bring new territories to explore, new supplies to gather, new threats to eliminate. The routine never changed, only the variables within it. Calculate, execute, survive. No other outcomes were acceptable.

As her consciousness began to fade, snowflakes drifted past the small window, coating the world outside in unmarked white. By morning, her tracks would be gone. No one would know she had passed through. No one would be following.

Just as she preferred it.

Somewhere, in a house with a smoking chimney, a man nursed a dislocated shoulder, a reminder that strangers were never to be trusted. And that, too, was a calculation of sorts—one whose answer she already knew.

Ed Rodriguez

No Horizon: Surface Tension

The waterline marked everything now. A dark, horizontal scar across the face of once-proud buildings, it divided the world into two realms: above and below. Both equally dangerous, just in different ways.

She studied the flooded downtown through her binoculars from atop an abandoned highway overpass. Three miles of submerged urban maze stretched between her and the military installation on the other side. Intelligence gathered from scattered survivor outposts suggested the base might still contain medical supplies, ammunition, and—most critically—batteries. Worth the risk, if the information was reliable. A proposition that remained doubtful at best.

99

Lowering the binoculars, she adjusted the waterproof pack containing her essentials: shotgun shells nestled in protective cases, fire-starting materials sealed in triple-layered plastic, water purification tablets, jerky, and other survival necessities. Her pump shotgun was secured across her back with paracord fashioned into a quick-release system. The machete and handaxe hung from her belt, their handles wrapped in grip tape to prevent slippage in wet conditions. The crowbar was strapped to the outside of her pack, while her survival knife remained in its ankle sheath, accessible even while swimming.

She unfolded a laminated city map marked with potential routes and danger zones. The eastern approach to the base featured the shallowest waters but would force her through a commercial district likely teeming with infected. The western approach offered deeper water—easier swimming, harder wading—but required navigating a complex of connected office buildings. The central approach, straight through the flood zone, was shortest but meant extended periods in open water with limited cover.

Central route it was. Tactical disadvantages aside, time was equally precious as ammunition. Daylight didn't last forever.

She descended from the overpass and approached the water's edge cautiously. The murky floodwater lapped at crumbled asphalt, carrying the faint metallic smell of industrial pollutants. Before entering, she applied a layer of petroleum jelly to exposed skin—a barrier against waterborne pathogens and extended immersion damage. From her pack came a pair of neoprene gloves, offering protection while maintaining dexterity.

Testing the water temperature with one gloved hand, she estimated she had approximately four hours before hypothermia became a concern. Sufficient time if no unforeseen complications arose. An unrealistic expectation given her experiences thus far.

She removed a small inflatable bladder from her pack and pumped it with fifteen quick breaths. Not large enough to support her entire body, but sufficient to keep her pack and shotgun dry while swimming. With habitual precision, she secured her most critical gear to the flotation device using a system of carabiners and quick-release knots.

The water reached mid-chest when she first entered, moving in a slow, controlled wade to minimize noise and splashing. Each step came with careful foot placement, testing for underwater obstacles or sudden dropoffs. The technique reduced speed but prevented ankle injuries that could prove fatal in this environment.

Two blocks in, the street dipped, and the water level rose to her shoulders. She transitioned to a modified combat sidestroke—one arm pulling through the water while the other guided the flotation device alongside. The technique allowed her to maintain situational awareness above the waterline while moving efficiently.

Movement to her right sent her instantly into stillness. Several infected shambled along a second-story walkway connecting office buildings. Their jerky movements and blood-crusted faces marked them as rabid—mindless, aggressive, driven purely by rage and hunger. Unlike the reanimated dead, they could still swim if they caught sight of prey.

She remained motionless until they passed, controlling her breathing to minimize ripples on the water's surface. Only after they disappeared into a shattered window did she resume her advance, now angling toward a partially submerged city bus that offered a route of covered movement.

The bus interior reeked of mold and decay. She climbed inside through a broken window, careful not to cut herself on the jagged glass. Water filled the vehicle to just below the seats, which she used as elevated platforms to rest and reassess her route.

Through the fractured windshield, she spotted an apartment building with an accessible fire escape. Moving there would allow elevation above the water level and faster progress across rooftops before needing to submerge again. She checked her waterproof watch—forty minutes had passed. Acceptable progress.

As she prepared to exit the bus, voices drifted through the broken windows. She froze, then slowly shifted to a position offering concealment while maintaining sightlines to the street.

Four survivors awkwardly navigated the flooded avenue in a makeshift raft constructed from interior doors lashed together with extension cords. Their voices carried across the water as they argued about direction and paddling technique. One wielded a baseball bat wrapped in barbed wire, another clutched a hunting rifle with a scope ill-suited for close-quarter combat. The third carried a crowbar similar to her own, while the fourth appeared unarmed. None wore appropriate water gear, their clothes saturated and heavy.

Amateurs. Dangerous not through malice but incompetence.

She watched them pass her position, deliberately remaining concealed. Their raft drifted toward an intersection she knew concealed a deep drainage channel—an unexpected dropoff that would capsize their improvised craft and plunge them into fifteen feet of water.

Staying in the bus meant safety. Logical choice. She turned away from the window, moving toward the rear emergency exit that would allow her to continue her journey in the opposite direction.

The first scream came exactly as anticipated. Then another, followed by frantic splashing and panicked shouts. Their makeshift raft had found the drainage channel, just as she'd foreseen.

She exited the bus silently, angling away from the commotion. Their misfortune was regrettable but not her concern. Survival required focus on immediate objectives, not rescuing strangers who lacked basic situational awareness.

The apartment building with the fire escape remained her target. She swam toward it with measured strokes, maintaining distance from the ongoing chaos behind her.

Halfway to her destination, the water erupted twenty feet ahead. Several infected burst into view, drawn by the survivors' distress. They thrashed forward with uncoordinated but determined movements, bypassing her position as they homed in on the louder targets.

More splashing from her left. Two undead emerging from a submerged storefront. The noise had drawn them from hiding places throughout the flooded district.

She changed course, moving perpendicular to both threats. The apartment building was temporarily unreachable. She redirected toward a low-rise parking structure whose second level stood above the waterline.

The infected closed on the struggling survivors. Their screams intensified, then abruptly ceased as one went under. The others continued fighting, one firing wildly with the hunting rifle, creating more noise that would only draw additional threats.

She reached the parking structure, pulling herself onto a concrete ramp with economical grace. From this elevated position, she assessed the deteriorating situation. The survivors were now separated, their raft capsized. One had already gone under. Another was being dragged beneath the surface by an infected that had latched onto his leg. The remaining two fought back-to-back, one swinging the barbed-wire bat in wide, panicked arcs.

Infected converged from multiple directions. Within minutes, the area would be overrun. The tactical solution was clear: allow the chaos to unfold, then navigate around the concentration of infected once they were occupied with the survivors.

Movement on her flank. An infected had spotted her, diverting from the main feeding frenzy to pursue this closer prey. It charged through the water with singular purpose, moving faster than its waterlogged condition should allow.

She drew her machete. Close-quarters combat was preferable to firing the shotgun and attracting more attention. As the infected reached the base of the ramp, she positioned herself at optimal striking distance, calculating its momentum.

It lunged upward with rabid ferocity, jaws snapping at air

as she sidestepped. The machete came down in a practiced arc, separating its head from shoulders in a single clean stroke. The body collapsed, creating barely a splash as it slid back into the flood.

Another appeared behind it. Then two more. The commotion had created a split in the horde, some still focused on the survivors, others now aware of her presence.

She retreated up the ramp, creating distance while maintaining dominant position. The infected followed, their movements hampered by the incline and water-logged clothing.

Three rapid machete strikes dispatched the first wave. The second required her to switch to the handaxe when one closed too quickly for the longer blade. The axe embedded in its skull with a wet crunch, requiring a sharp twist to free the weapon.

From the water below, the bearded man with the crowbar had spotted her. He shouted something, gesturing frantically as he tried to swim toward the parking structure. The older woman followed, abandoning the bat-wielding survivor who had already been surrounded.

She had no obligation to assist. Their poor planning had created this disaster. But the infected were now divided between targets, creating tactical opportunity. More importantly, the route to her objective was temporarily blocked by the concentrated activity near the drainage channel. Allowing some survivors to reach her position might divide the infected further, improving her odds of advancing.

She made no welcoming gesture but didn't prevent them from climbing the ramp to join her. The bearded man arrived first, soaked and gasping for breath. The older woman followed moments later, surprisingly composed despite the exertion.

"Thank you," the man wheezed. "We thought—"

She cut him off with a sharp gesture toward the ongoing carnage in the water. The hat-wielding survivor had gone under. The fourth member of their group was nowhere to be seen. Infected still swarmed the area, some now noticing the survivors who had escaped to the parking structure.

"Move," she snarled, her voice rough and dry. She pointed toward the upper levels of the parking structure, where a pedestrian bridge connected to a nearby office building.

They followed without argument, the bearded man retrieving his crowbar from a loop on his belt. The older woman produced a knife from inside her boot—the only sign of preparedness she'd demonstrated thus far.

On the third level, she paused to reassess their position. The infected below had begun following the ramp upward, but their progress was slow. The pedestrian bridge offered escape to the office building, which might provide access to the apartment complex she'd originally targeted.

"I'm Adam," the bearded man said, extending his hand. "This is—"

"Don't care," she interrupted, turning away to check the bridge's stability. Names created attachments. Attachments created vulnerabilities.

The older woman snorted. "Smart girl."

The pedestrian bridge had partially collapsed, creating a steep incline but remaining traversable. She led them across in single file, testing each step before committing her weight. The bearded man—Adam—followed too closely, nearly losing his footing when a section gave way beneath him.

Inside the office building, cubicles and conference rooms offered multiple pathways. She navigated by maintaining orientation toward the apartment complex visible through eastern windows. The survivors followed in silence, the older woman occasionally pausing to gather potentially useful items: a letter opener, a roll of tape, painkillers from a desk drawer.

As they reached a sky bridge connecting to the apartment complex, a crash sounded from the floor below. Then another. Infected had entered the building.

"We should run," Adam whispered, peering nervously over the stairwell railing.

She shook her head, pointing to the sky bridge. Running created noise. Noise attracted infected. Move quickly but deliberately.

They crossed the sky bridge into a residential hallway lined with apartment doors. Most stood ajar, their interiors long since looted for valuables. She selected one with an intact door, shepherding the survivors inside before securing the entrance with a wooden chair wedged under the handle.

From the apartment window, she could see the military base in the distance. Progress toward her objective had been minimal, largely due to the detour caused by the survivors' incompetence.

Adam joined her at the window. "We're trying to reach the old stadium on the east side. Heard there's a community there."

She made no response. Rumors of safe havens inevitably proved false. People clung to such myths out of desperate need for hope, not evidence.

The older woman rummaged through kitchen cabinets, finding only dust and roach droppings. "Nothing here. Picked clean." Her matter-of-fact tone suggested long experience with disappointment.

A thud against the apartment door. Then scratching. The infected had tracked them.

She drew her shotgun. The situation had deteriorated beyond stealth considerations. The chair wouldn't hold if multiple infected concentrated their efforts on the door.

"Back exit?" Adam asked, raising his crowbar.

She pointed to the bathroom window that opened onto a narrow ledge connecting to the adjacent apartment. Not ideal, but preferable to confronting an unknown number of infected in confined quarters.

The older woman went first, her weathered frame displaying surprising agility as she navigated the ledge. Adam followed, less gracefully but successfully. As the door began splintering inward, she slipped through the window and pulled it shut behind her.

They made their way through several connected apartments before finding a service stairwell. Descending to the second floor put them just above the waterline, where fallen ceiling tiles and rotted carpeting squished underfoot.

Adam checked his watch. "Few hours of daylight left. We should—"

A crash from beyond the stairwell door interrupted him. The infected had burst through from the adjoining corridor. Three of them charged forward, their rage-contorted faces and bloody clothes identifying them as recently turned.

She raised her shotgun, firing once. The lead infected's head disappeared in a spray of bone and tissue. The second met the same fate a moment later. The third reached Adam before she could chamber another round.

His crowbar caught it in the throat, momentarily halting its advance. The older woman lunged with her knife, but her strike was slightly off-center. The infected twisted violently, its jaws snapping at her exposed forearm before her blade found its temple. The creature collapsed instantly.

But the encounter had cost them. The older woman cried

out, clutching her arm where the infected's teeth had torn flesh. Blood welled between her fingers, dripping onto the sodden carpet.

"Just a scratch," she insisted, though her pallor suggested otherwise. "Barely broke skin."

She stepped forward, examining the wound critically. Teeth marks clearly penetrated the flesh. Any saliva contact with broken skin or mucous membranes was sufficient. The older woman was infected.

"Kill me," the older woman said immediately, her tone eerily calm. "I know what happens."

Adam stepped between them. "Wait. We can find medicine, maybe—"

The older woman laughed harshly. "Don't be stupid. There's no cure for a bite." She turned to her. "You know what needs doing."

She nodded, raising her pistol. Adam tried to intervene, but the older woman pushed him aside with surprising strength.

115

"Rather go out on my terms," the woman said. "Not as one of those things."

Adam looked away as the gunshot echoed through the empty building. The older woman's body collapsed against the wall, a neat hole centered in her forehead. A mercy only possible because she'd recognized reality.

"Move," she said, voice flat. "Noise brings more."

Adam stared at his companion's body, shock evident on his face. "She was my friend. Her name was—"

"Doesn't matter now," she interrupted. Names changed nothing. The dead were dead.

They continued toward the military base, now using exterior balconies to navigate above the floodwater. Adam remained silent, occasionally glancing back toward the building where they'd left the older woman's body.

Two hours later, they reached the edge of the military compound. Night was approaching, and they'd need to find shelter soon. A chain-link fence topped with razor wire encircled the perimeter, much of it now submerged. The main gate had been barricaded with transport vehicles, creating an improvised wall that had partially collapsed.

They entered through a drainage culvert, wading through chest-deep water before emerging inside the compound. Bodies in military fatigues littered the ground, most showing head wounds inflicted after death.

They took shelter in a secure guard post for the night. She positioned herself by the single entrance, shotgun across her lap, refusing Adam's offer to take shifts. Trust was a luxury she couldn't afford. Adam tossed restlessly in the corner, grief and fear preventing real sleep. She remained vigilant until dawn, when they resumed their exploration.

The central command building stood relatively intact, its windows dark and uninviting. She approached cautiously, signaling Adam to cover the rear. Learned behavior, at least. Perhaps he wasn't entirely hopeless.

Inside, emergency lighting cast weak red illumination

117

across blood-spattered corridors. No movement disturbed the silence. The installation had been abandoned for months, possibly longer.

The operations center contained the anticipated supplies: ammunition boxes stacked in corners, medical supplies in steel cabinets, batteries still in protective packaging. The evacuation had been hasty, prioritizing personnel over equipment.

While Adam gathered batteries and medical supplies, she found situational reports documenting the base's final days:

Day 17: Perimeter breached in multiple locations. Charlie Company dispatched to restore containment. Seven casualties, including Captain Johnson.

Day 21: Half of barracks now serving as isolation zones. Infection spreading despite precautions. Command structure fragmenting as regional HQ goes silent.

Day 23: General Davis led remaining combat-effective personnel to secondary facility. Volunteer skeleton crew remaining to maintain communications and assist civilian evacuation.

Day 25: Last civilian convoy departed 0600. Remaining personnel authorized to withdraw. God help those left behind.

The final entry, scrawled in shaking handwriting: *They're inside. No way out. If you find this, don't waste time searching. Nothing left worth dying for.*

"Oh shit!" Adam gasped aloud.

He had found a younger man hiding beneath an overturned desk. Dirty, terrified, but unbitten. The missing fourth member of their group who had somehow made his way to the military base independently. Her eyes narrowed with suspicion.

"Tom! You made it!" Adam embraced him, relief evident in his voice. "We thought you were dead."

Tom shook visibly, words tumbling out in disconnected fragments. "Swam... under them... hid in a truck..." He clutched Adam's sleeve. "Tried for the stadium first... too many infected... saw the base towers instead... they're everywhere now... heard the shots..."

119

The young man's erratic behavior raised immediate concerns. She stepped closer, examining him for bite marks or other signs of infection.

"I'm fine," Tom insisted, noticing her scrutiny. "Just cold. Been hiding here since yesterday, after the water carried me away from you guys."

Adam wrapped a blanket around his shoulders, then resumed gathering supplies. "We'll get you warm. Found some food too."

She remained watchful. The young man's pupils seemed overly dilated, his skin flushed despite claims of coldness. Classic early-stage infection indicators.

Thirty minutes later, her suspicions proved correct. Tom collapsed while sorting medical supplies, his body suddenly wracked with convulsions. Adam rushed to his side, cradling his head.

"What's happening? Tom!"

She drew her handaxe. "Bitten." No question in her tone.

"No, he said he wasn't—"

"Lying," she stated flatly, gesturing to Tom's deteriorating condition. His skin had developed a grayish pallor, veins darkening beneath the surface. Eyes clouding rapidly.

"Get away from him," she warned, her voice low but urgent. "Now."

Adam still didn't move away. "We can help him. The medical supplies—"

Tom's body went suddenly rigid, then relaxed completely. For ten seconds, nothing happened. Then his eyes opened— vacant, yet somehow hungry.

He lunged upward with inhuman speed, teeth sinking into Adam's neck before either could react. Blood sprayed across the console as Adam screamed, trying to push the infected away.

Her axe came down in a practiced arc, embedding in Tom's skull with a wet crunch. The body collapsed sideways, twitching briefly before going still.

Adam clutched his neck, blood flowing between his

fingers. "Oh god," he whispered, reality finally registering. "I'm bit."

She nodded, expression unchanged. Another inevitable outcome.

"How long?" he asked, sliding down against the wall.

"Hours." Sometimes less, depending on bite location and individual physiology. Neck bites progressed rapidly due to proximity to the brain.

He nodded, resignation replacing panic. "Will you...?"

She understood. Another mercy killing when the time came. She inclined her head slightly.

Adam removed a worn photo from his pocket. Two children smiled back, a boy and girl perhaps six and eight years old. "My kids. At their mom's when it started. Never found out what..." His voice trailed off.

She gathered supplies while he deteriorated, categorizing and packing items based on utility and weight. The military base had yielded significant resources: ammunition compatible with her weapons, medical supplies including antibiotics, batteries, and water purification tablets.

Adam's condition worsened rapidly. Within two hours, his skin had developed the telltale gray pallor, veins darkening beneath the surface. The wound on his neck had turned black at the edges, infection spreading visibly through surrounding tissue.

"It's time," he said, voice barely above a whisper. "Please."

She nodded, drawing her pistol and chambering a round. Clean. Quick. Necessary.

"Wait," he rasped. "My last name... someone should remember..."

She shook her head. Names didn't matter. Only actions remained after death.

Understanding crossed his features. He nodded once, closing his eyes.

The gunshot echoed through the empty command center.

She exited the military base as daylight faded, carrying

her expanded inventory in a reconfigured pack. The flood waters reflected sunset colors, creating an almost beautiful tableau disconnected from the death and decay it concealed.

On her laminated map, she marked the military base as depleted of useful resources. Her next objective would be the highlands to the northwest, where a fallback site designated "Echo Site" had been established in a former mining complex, according to the military reports.

No guarantee it still existed. No assurance anyone survived there. But movement remained preferable to stagnation.

She found shelter for the night in a rooftop mechanical room overlooking the flood zone. The military base was visible in the distance, a dark silhouette against the marginally lighter horizon. No movement disturbed its outlines. No lights appeared in its windows. Just another monument to failed civilization.

From her elevated position, she could see for miles across the flooded city. No artificial lights broke the darkness. No signals suggested other survivors. Just water and ruins stretching toward a horizon that promised nothing.

As she arranged her supplies with methodical precision, the faces of today's dead briefly crossed her memory: the older woman, accepting reality with dignity; Adam, clutching a photograph of children he would never see again; Tom, lost to infection and madness. All gone, like countless others before them.

She allowed herself twenty minutes of rest before preparing for the following day's journey. Survival required nothing more than continuing forward. No hope necessary. No companionship required. Just constant adaptation to an environment that offered no reprieve and no forgiveness.

She cleaned her weapons by the fading light, movements practiced to the point of ritual. Tomorrow would bring new threats, new challenges, new decisions.

For now, she had shelter, supplies, and silence.

It was enough.

Ed Rodriguez

No Horizon: Fever Dreams

The fever made her hands shake.

She pressed her palm against the gash on her thigh, wincing as fresh blood seeped between her fingers. The makeshift bandage—a torn shirt sleeve—had soaked through completely. Bad sign. The wound wasn't deep enough to hit an artery, but the infection was taking hold.

Three days since she'd caught her leg on that jagged metal support beam while fleeing through a collapsing warehouse. The rusted edge had sliced clean through her pants and deep into the muscle. Rookie mistake. She knew better.

She'd cleaned it as best she could then, but hadn't dared

stop long enough for proper suturing with the infected in pursuit. Now the wound was paying the price.

The abandoned ranger station overlooking the valley offered temporary sanctuary—brick construction, metal roof, and most importantly, only one door and two windows to secure. She'd dragged a heavy desk across the door after picking the lock. The windows were already boarded from the outside, with enough gaps between planks to monitor the surroundings.

Her vision blurred as she emptied her backpack onto the dusty floor. Water bottles—two full, one half-empty. Canned beans. Beef jerky. First aid kit, nearly depleted. She found the small bottle of antibiotics—three pills remaining. The label had worn off long ago, but she recognized the shape and color. Broad-spectrum. Better than nothing.

She swallowed one pill dry, grimacing at the bitter taste. Conserve water. Always conserve water.

The ranger's desk yielded a half-bottle of whiskey in the bottom drawer. Good. She poured a measure over the wound, biting down on her leather belt to muffle her scream. The pain came in waves, each one threatening to drag her under.

With trembling hands, she threaded the curved needle from her kit. The stitches were ugly but functional, pulling the ragged edges of the wound together. The whiskey made for a poor antiseptic, but it was better than nothing. She packed the wound with crushed antibacterial herbs she'd collected last week, then wrapped it with a fresh bandage torn from a reasonably clean sheet found in a storage closet.

Her eyelids grew heavy as she propped herself against the wall, shotgun across her lap, machete within reach. Just a short rest. She couldn't afford more.

Sleep came anyway, pulling her down into fever dreams of fire and blood.

The university library had been her salvation that first day.

She'd been finalizing lecture notes for her environmental

biology class when the first screams echoed through the stacks. The initial reports had been vague—a new strain of rabies, they said. Highly contagious. Isolated cases.

They lied.

From the third-floor window, she watched civilization unravel in less than an hour. People running, bleeding. Others attacking with inhuman ferocity, teeth and fingernails their only weapons. Campus security overwhelmed in minutes.

Her research on ecosystem collapse and biological adaptation strategies suddenly seemed like cruel foreshadowing. For years, she'd lectured on how quickly natural systems could destabilize past certain tipping points. Now she was witnessing societal collapse in real-time.

Fire alarms blared as smoke began filling the corridors. Someone had set fires, either deliberately or in the chaos.

She'd grabbed her backpack, hands trembling as she dumped textbooks to make room for bottled water and protein bars from a vending machine she'd smashed with a fire extinguisher. It had taken three awkward swings before the glass finally shattered.

The administrative office yielded a letter opener—a poor weapon, but better than nothing. She held it uncertainly, the weight unfamiliar in her hand.

Her mind calculated options with academic precision even as her body betrayed her with tremors. Ground floor exits were overrun. Fire escape on the east side. Possible. If she moved quietly. Something she'd read about predator avoidance in prey species. Move perpendicular to the threat's line of sight. Stay downwind. Theory, now life-or-death practice.

The stairwell door opened to screams and wet sounds of violence one floor below. She closed it with fumbling fingers, heart hammering against her ribs. Not that way.

The smoke was getting thicker. She tied her scarf over her nose and mouth, staying low. Her glasses kept slipping down her sweat-slicked nose.

A university maintenance worker stumbled through the

door at the far end of the corridor. His coveralls were soaked with blood, eyes wild with fever. He spotted her and charged, howling.

She tried to sidestep but misjudged the timing. They collided, tumbling to the floor in a tangle of limbs. The letter opener was knocked from her grasp, skittering across the linoleum. Panic rose in her throat as his weight pinned her down, his fevered strength overwhelming.

His teeth snapped inches from her face. In desperate reflex, she jammed her forearm under his chin, pushing back with surprising strength born of terror. Her free hand scrabbled for the letter opener, fingers brushing its handle just beyond reach.

With a guttural cry, she bucked her hips and rolled, momentarily throwing him off balance. It was enough. Her fingers closed around the letter opener, and she swung blindly.

The blade found the soft spot beneath his jaw, driving upward with more luck than skill. His body convulsed once, then went still.

Blood covered her hands. The first life she'd taken. She

retched, emptying her stomach against the wall, tears mingling with sweat and ash.

The faculty lounge yielded better weapons—a heavy flashlight and a box cutter with fresh blades. From the window, she could see the fire escape two rooms down. The building's fire suppression system finally activated, sprinklers raining down tepid water that mixed with the smoke into a choking fog.

A crash from behind. A group of infected burst through the double doors, their movements jerky and uncoordinated but terrifyingly fast. She hurled a chair through the window, glass shattering outward, cutting her palm in the process.

The infected rushed her as she climbed onto the sill, nearly losing her balance. One grabbed her ankle. She kicked wildly, connecting with its face. The grip loosened just enough for her to pull free. She jumped to the fire escape landing, metal rattling beneath her weight, ankle twisting as she landed awkwardly.

The infected followed, clambering through the window

with no regard for the broken glass shredding their palms and knees. She descended as fast as she dared, the metal staircase slick with rain, her injured ankle protesting with each step.

Ground level brought new dangers—a small crowd of infected milled about the alley. The commotion from above drew their attention. Heads snapped up in unison, a grotesque choreography of hunger.

She ran the opposite direction, towards the street, her gait uneven and clumsy. A police car burned on the corner, no sign of its occupants. The campus quad had become a killing field, infected swarming those too slow to escape.

The streets were chaos incarnate. She navigated them with growing dread, each block taking her closer to home. She had to reach them. Had to know.

Her home was silent when she finally arrived.
"Hello?" Her voice sounded alien to her own ears.

The living room was undisturbed. The kitchen showed signs of a hasty meal—a coffee cup still half-full, breakfast dishes on the counter.

A wet, dragging sound came from down the hall.

She moved toward it, box cutter extended before her like a talisman. The bedroom door was partially closed. She pushed it open with her foot.

What she found inside destroyed any hope she'd maintained during her desperate journey home. The scene burned itself into her memory—blood-soaked bedding, movement in the shadows, the snarling thing that had once been beloved turning toward her with hungry, feverish eyes.

She fled.

The fever dream shifted. Fragments of a life dismantled— photographs blurred by tears and rain, a child's toy abandoned in a rush to escape, a gold band she'd eventually removed when the weight of it became too much to bear.

Time fractured, memories collapsing into one another. Nearly a year after the collapse.

She lay on a military cot, bandages wrapped around her

midsection. The make-shift clinic had once been a veterinary office. Medical supplies were organized with meticulous care on shelves once meant for pet food and flea treatments.

"You're lucky," the doctor said, adjusting her IV drip. His beard was neatly trimmed despite the apocalypse, his eyes kind behind wire-rimmed glasses. "The knife missed anything vital. But the infection was setting in. Another day, you might have been beyond help."

She'd been ambushed by two men while scavenging a pharmacy. One had stabbed her before she could bring her shotgun to bear. She'd managed to kill them both, but the wound had weakened her. The doctor had found her collapsed in an alley behind his clinic.

"Why help me?" she asked, voice rough from disuse. The first words she'd spoken to another person in months.

He shrugged. "Same reason I became a doctor before all this. Someone has to."

His name was Michael. He'd been an emergency room

physician. When the pandemic hit, he'd worked until the hospital was overrun, then escaped with as many supplies as he could carry.

"Most people don't know how to properly clean a wound," he told her, changing her bandages with well-honed technique. "Or which antibiotics work for what. Or how to recognize the early signs of infection before it becomes systemic."

Over the weeks of her recovery, he taught her. The proper way to irrigate a wound. How to suture different types of lacerations. Which medications could be substituted for others when supplies ran low. How to perform basic surgical procedures under field conditions.

"Knowledge is the most valuable resource now," he said one evening as they shared a meal of canned stew warmed over a small alcohol burner. "It weighs nothing. Can't be stolen unless they take your life too."

She found herself talking to him. Small things at first. Then, one night, about what had happened at home. The words came haltingly, painful as lancing a wound.

He listened without interruption, then shared his own loss —a fiancée who'd been on a flight that never landed after air traffic control systems collapsed.

They weren't friends, exactly. The word seemed inadequate for survivors sharing the end of the world. But there was trust. A rare commodity.

The infected came at dawn, a massive group of at least thirty. Later, she would wonder if they'd been drawn by the small generator Michael ran occasionally to power essential medical equipment.

The clinic had defensible positions—barred windows, reinforced doors. But not against so many. The barricades failed within minutes.

The front door splintered under the weight of the horde. She grabbed the shotgun, firing at the first infected that stumbled through. Two shells, two bodies down. But more kept coming.

"There are too many!" Michael shouted, wielding a fire

axe he kept by the door. He swung it in a wide arc, catching an infected in the shoulder. The blow didn't stop it.

She fired again, the blast taking the infected's head clean off. Three shells left. Twenty more infected pushing through the doorway.

Michael backed toward her, swinging the axe defensively. "We need to go out the back. Now!"

They retreated toward the rear exit, firing and swinging in desperate coordination. She reloaded with shaking hands, fumbling a shell that clattered to the floor.

They almost made it.

Multiple infected lunged through a side window that gave way under their combined weight. They grabbed Michael before he could bring the axe around, dragging him to the ground in a tangle of grasping hands and snapping teeth.

"Michael!" She fired the shotgun, taking down one of his attackers, but the others were already tearing at him.

She grabbed his outstretched hand, trying to pull him free.

For a moment, their eyes met. Blood bubbled from his mouth.

"Go!" he gasped, pushing her away with his remaining strength. "Blue backpack... by the door... take it..."

More infected poured in from the front. They would be on her in seconds.

"GO!" Michael screamed one final time as teeth found his throat.

The rational choice was clear. She could not save him. Stay and die. Or go and live.

She grabbed the blue backpack by the rear exit and fled into the alley, the sounds of Michael's final screams following her. Quick, then abruptly silenced. The doctor who had saved her, who had taught her to save herself, was gone.

She ran without looking back, the weight of the medical supplies a reminder of what his sacrifice had purchased. Her survival.

That night, sheltered in an abandoned storage unit, she meticulously inventoried the backpack's contents. Antibiotics.

Surgical tools. Painkillers. Bandages. All labeled in his neat handwriting.

She memorized every item, every use. Knowledge. The resource that couldn't be stolen.

The fever dream shifted again. More than a year after the collapse.

She'd learned that the infected eventually died from their condition—brains burning out from the constant rage and exertion. But death wasn't the end. They reanimated, slower but relentless, driven by a different hunger.

The undead were easier to avoid but harder to kill. Only head trauma stopped them permanently.

She discovered this in an abandoned gas station when she encountered an old reanimated corpse. The shotgun blast to its chest did nothing. It kept coming, arms outstretched, jaw working silently. The second blast removed its head, ending the threat.

Valuable lesson, costly in ammunition. The machete

141

became her primary weapon against the undead—quieter and more efficient once she learned proper striking angles for the skull.

By then, she'd acquired a handaxe from a rural hardware store. The perfect multi-purpose tool—hammer side for construction and breaking, blade side for cutting and splitting. Small enough to hang from her belt, heavy enough to crush a skull.

She was learning, adapting. Each day brought new challenges, new lessons. Sleep in shifts. Trust nothing. No fire at night. Always have an escape route. Water before food. Food before shelter. Shelter before rest.

The professor she had once been would be fascinated by her adaptation, by the evolutionary pressure of apocalypse selecting for certain traits. The human she had been would be horrified by what necessity had made of her.

She was neither now. Just a survivor.

The family photo she'd carried for the first year had

disintegrated from frequent handling, until she'd finally burned the remains. Their faces were etched in her memory anyway. Better not to leave personal artifacts that might slow her down or compromise operational security.

Never make the same mistake twice.

Daylight filtered through the boarded windows when she opened her eyes.

The fever had broken during the night. Her leg throbbed, but the angry red streaks had receded. The antibiotics and whiskey had done their job.

She tested her weight on the injured leg. Painful but functional. She rebandaged the wound with methodical precision, mentally thanking Michael for knowledge that had saved her life countless times.

She packed her supplies systematically. The ranger station had been a good temporary shelter, but staying in one place invited disaster.

The desk drawer contained a state park map, which she studied carefully. A visitors' center ten miles north might have more medical supplies. Beyond that, mountains offered defensive positions and hunting opportunities.

She loaded the shotgun and secured the machete to her pack. She held the crowbar at her side, ready to use as both weapon and support when navigating difficult terrain, taking some pressure off her injured leg.

Before leaving, she swept the station for any overlooked supplies. A forgotten multi-tool in another desk drawer. A rain poncho folded in a filing cabinet. A half-empty box of ammunition that didn't fit her shotgun but might be valuable for trade if she ever encountered friendly survivors.

Unlikely. But possible.

She checked the perimeter through gaps in the boarded windows, confirming no immediate threats. The morning fog provided additional cover. Good conditions for travel.

With seasoned proficiency, she shouldered her pack,

adjusted the weight distribution, and opened the door just wide enough to slip through. The metal latch made barely a sound as she pulled it shut behind her.

The dirt path leading away from the station disappeared into mist. No horizon visible. Just the next step, then the one after that.

She moved forward, as she always did. No looking back. No hesitation.

Survival was the only objective that mattered.

Ed Rodriguez

No Horizon: Cold Calculus

The shotgun's weight against her shoulder felt like an old friend. She held her breath, aimed, and squeezed the trigger. The infected's head disappeared in a spray of red, its body collapsing mid-stride.

One shell, one kill.

She worked the pump, ejecting the spent shell as she pivoted, tracking the second infected through the iron sights. Another controlled breath. Another squeeze. Another body on the ground.

Two shells, two kills.

The third infected was too close. She slung the shotgun and drew her machete in one fluid motion, stepping aside as the creature lunged past her. Its momentum carried it forward, exposing its back. She buried the blade at the base of its skull, severing the brain stem. The body dropped, twitching.

No ammunition wasted. No unnecessary noise. Just the efficient application of force.

She pulled the machete free, wiped the blade on the infected's clothing, and returned it to the sheath at her hip. Three threats neutralized in less than fifteen seconds. Not her best time, but adequate.

The street looked clear now. She retrieved the spent shotgun shells and tucked them into a pouch. Empty brass could be reloaded if she found the necessary components. Nothing went to waste anymore.

The pharmacy had been picked clean of medications long ago, but the stockroom might still contain overlooked supplies. She slipped through the back entrance, crowbar at the ready. The door yielded with minimal resistance, hinges protesting after years of disuse.

Inside, darkness reigned. She produced a small flashlight from her pocket, holding it alongside the crowbar in her left hand —a technique that preserved her dominant hand for defense while providing illumination. The beam cut through the gloom, revealing shelves of knocked-over products and a floor littered with packaging.

She moved methodically through the space, her footfalls nearly silent. Years of practice had taught her how to distribute her weight, how to test each step before committing to it. A loose floorboard or displaced piece of debris could alert nearby threats.

In the far corner, she spotted what she was after: a fallen shelving unit that would have been too heavy for most scavengers to move. Potential. She secured the flashlight between her teeth and set to work with the crowbar, leveraging the metal shelving unit enough to create a gap.

Behind it, as she'd hoped, sat a small stockpile of overlooked supplies: gauze bandages, antiseptic, medical tape. Most valuable of all, a half-dozen bottles of antibiotics. Silent gold in a world where infection meant death.

She packed the supplies carefully into her backpack, organizing them by type and priority of use. Order mattered. In a crisis, fumbling through a disorganized pack could mean the difference between survival and death.

The building groaned around her, shifting in the wind. She froze, listening. Not wind. Footsteps on the floor above. Heavy, deliberate. Human.

Raiders.

She extinguished the flashlight and waited, letting her eyes readjust to the darkness. Unlike the infected, humans were unpredictable. Dangerous. They thought, planned, and adapted. They used guns and set traps. They hunted.

She positioned herself in a corner with a view of both the back exit and the stairwell. The shotgun would be too loud, attracting every infected in a three-block radius. She unsheathed her survival knife instead. Quiet. Effective at close range. Versatile.

The footsteps moved toward the stairwell. She tightened her grip on the knife, muscle memory finding the optimal balance point. One raider she could handle silently. More would complicate things.

A beam of light preceded the figure down the stairs— sloppy tactics. The light ruined the raider's night vision while telegraphing his position. Amateur.

She remained motionless as he reached the bottom of the stairs, sweeping his light across the stockroom. His back was to her, a silhouette against the flashlight's glow. She could end him now, quickly and quietly. One less threat in a world full of them.

The light paused, then swung back to illuminate a small object on the floor. The raider bent down, picking up one of the empty medication boxes she'd discarded.

"Hello?" His voice cracked, barely above a whisper. "Is someone here? I'm not looking for trouble."

She didn't respond. Words were unnecessary. Dangerous, even. Sound attracted the infected and revealed positions to hostiles.

"Please," he continued, "my sister's sick. Bad infection. She needs medicine."

The knife remained steady in her hand. His story was irrelevant. Could be true. Could be bait. Either way, attachment was a luxury she couldn't afford. The calculus was simple: her survival against uncertain outcomes.

The raider moved further into the room, the beam of his flashlight dancing across the floor. "I saw the fresh tracks outside. I know someone's here."

His observation skills were better than she'd given him credit for. She shifted slightly, preparing to strike if he came closer.

Then she heard it. The soft shuffle of feet outside the building. The distinctive guttural moan of the reanimated. The dead were coming, drawn by the raider's voice.

He heard it too, tensing visibly. "Shit," he hissed, fumbling with a holstered pistol.

If he fired that gun, every infected within hearing distance would converge on this location. The smart play was to let him die, creating a distraction while she slipped out the back.

But the antibiotics in her pack were enough for two. Possibly the difference between life and death for a sick girl somewhere.

The cold calculus faltered.

"Back exit," she whispered, breaking her silence. "Now."

The raider spun toward her voice, gun half-raised. She was already moving, grabbing his arm and directing the weapon toward the floor.

"Quiet," she hissed. "Back exit. Follow."

Understanding dawned in his eyes. He nodded and fell in behind her as she led the way through the stockroom, navigating the obstacle course of fallen shelves and scattered debris with practiced ease.

The moans grew louder. Multiple infected, converging on the pharmacy. She eased the back door open, scanning the alley beyond. Clear for now, but that would change quickly.

She gestured the raider through, then followed, pulling the door shut behind them. No time for stealth now. Speed was the priority.

"This way," the raider whispered, pointing toward a side street. "I have a safe house three blocks east."

She hesitated. Following him meant deviating from her planned route. Trusting a stranger. Breaking her own rules of survival.

But the antibiotics...

She reached into her pack and extracted two bottles, holding them out to him without a word.

The raider stared at the medication, then at her. "You're giving me these?"

In answer, she pressed the bottles into his hand and turned to go her own way. The transaction was complete. No further interaction necessary.

"Wait," he called, voice still low but urgent. "Please. It's not safe out there alone. We have food, clean water. A defensible position. Just for the night."

The logical choice was to disappear now, to stick to her plan. To survive as she had for years—alone, unencumbered, unburdened by others' needs or weaknesses.

Yet something tugged at her. Not sentiment—she'd burned that out of herself long ago—but perhaps a recognition of mutual advantage. Safety in numbers, if only temporarily. A chance to replenish supplies. To sleep with someone else standing watch.

She nodded once, gesturing for him to lead the way.

They moved through the streets in tandem, two shadows slipping between abandoned vehicles and crumbling buildings. The raider was surprisingly competent, choosing covered routes and maintaining awareness of their surroundings. Not an amateur after all.

Three blocks became five as they detoured around a cluster of infected. She dispatched one with her knife when it strayed too close, a swift thrust through the eye socket into the brain. The raider watched with a mixture of awe and unease.

"There," he whispered eventually, indicating a boarded-up townhouse at the end of the street. "We've reinforced the ground floor. Entry point is the second story."

He led her to a nearby garage with a fire escape ladder pulled down just enough to reach with a jump. Smart setup. Defensible. She approved of the tactical thinking.

Inside, the townhouse was spare but organized. Solar chargers for batteries. Rain collection system feeding into water purifiers. Dried food stored in rodent-proof containers. A makeshift medical station where a teenage girl lay on a cot, face flushed with fever.

"Ellie, I found medicine," the raider said, moving quickly to the girl's side. "And help."

She remained by the entry point, assessing the space, cataloging exits, evaluating threats and resources. Two more people emerged from adjoining rooms—an elderly man and a middle-aged woman. Both looked at her with a mixture of hope and suspicion.

"Thank you for helping my son," the older woman said. "I'm Kate. That's my daughter Ellie, and my father, James."

She nodded in acknowledgment but offered no name in return. Names were irrelevant. Attachments, dangerous.

"Please, sit," Kate continued, gesturing to a table where bowls of some kind of stew sat steaming. "You must be hungry."

Food could be drugged. People could be deceptive. But the setup looked legitimate, and they'd had ample opportunity to harm her already if that was their intent.

She set her pack down within easy reach and took a seat, keeping her back to the wall and her eyes on the room. The stew was rabbit and wild vegetables—simple but nourishing. She ate methodically, refueling her body while observing the family's dynamics.

The raider—Thomas, she learned—administered the antibiotics to his sister with careful precision, checking the dosage twice before helping her swallow the pills. The old man kept watch at the window, a lever-action rifle across his knees. Kate cleaned up the cooking area with methodical swiftness.

A functioning unit. Surviving through cooperation. An anomaly in a world where most groups had devolved into predatory gangs.

"You're welcome to stay," Kate said later, as darkness fell completely. "We take two-hour watch shifts through the night."

She considered the offer. One night of secure rest would be valuable. She could contribute to the watch rotation, assess their security protocols, possibly trade some of her medical supplies for food before moving on.

"I'll take first watch," she said, her voice rusty from disuse.

Kate nodded, unsurprised by her caution. "Second floor has the best sightlines. Thomas will show you."

The watch position was well-chosen—a corner room with windows facing two directions, much of the furniture removed to create clear lines of movement. Someone had constructed wooden shutters with narrow slits for observation, reducing light leakage while maintaining visibility.

She settled in with her shotgun across her lap, eyes scanning the darkened streets below. The town was relatively quiet tonight. A few lone infected wandered aimlessly. No signs of organized human activity.

Thomas joined her briefly, pointing out the pattern of signals they used—three taps for general alert, five rapid taps for immediate threat. Simple but effective.

"We haven't survived this long by being careless," he explained. "Everyone pulls their weight. Everyone contributes."

She nodded, recognizing the echo of her own philosophy. Efficiency. Pragmatism. No waste, no weakness.

"Why did you help me?" he asked suddenly. "You could have let me walk into those infected. Taken my gear after."

She considered the question. The answer wasn't clear even to her. Perhaps a momentary weakness. Perhaps a tactical calculation that helping him offered more advantage than harm.

"The antibiotics," she said finally. "Better used than wasted."

He studied her for a moment, then nodded. "Well, whatever the reason, thank you. Ellie's all I have left."

He left her to the watch then, returning downstairs to his sister. She resumed her vigilant scan of the surroundings, compartmentalizing the interaction. The family's dynamics were not her concern. Their survival was not her responsibility. Come morning, she would move on as planned.

The night passed uneventfully. She took her watch shift, then allowed herself four hours of light sleep, waking at the slightest sound. At dawn, she packed her gear, prepared to depart.

The family gathered to see her off. Thomas offered a package of dried meat and fruits. "For the road," he explained. "Fair trade for the medicine."

She accepted with a nod, tucking the provisions into her pack.

"Our door is open if you pass this way again," Kate said. "Sometimes it's good to have a place to return to."

The words stirred something long dormant. She'd had places once. People. Before the world died. Before survival became the only metric that mattered.

She shouldered her pack and headed for the exit. No goodbyes. No promises. Just the next step in an endless journey.

Two blocks from the townhouse, she heard it—the distinctive rumble of vehicles. Multiple engines, moving with purpose.

Raiders. Organized ones.

She melted into the shadow of a collapsed storefront, watching as three pickup trucks rolled slowly down the main street. Men with rifles stood in the beds, scanning buildings. A methodical search pattern. Hunting.

She could slip away now. Continue on her planned route. The family wasn't her responsibility.

But the raiders would find the townhouse eventually. The family's security was good against infected, not against coordinated human assault. They would be overwhelmed. Killed or worse.

The antibiotics would go to waste after all.

She circled back, moving swiftly through alleys and backyards. The raider patrol hadn't reached the townhouse yet, but their search pattern would bring them there within thirty minutes.

She found Thomas on watch, his expression shifting from surprise to alarm at her return.

"Raiders," she said without preamble. "Three vehicles. At least a dozen armed men. Searching systematically."

His face paled. "How long?"

"Not long. You need to evacuate. Now."

He nodded, turning to alert his family. Within minutes, they were gathering essential supplies, moving with the practiced urgency of people accustomed to emergency relocations.

"We have a fallback position," Thomas explained as he helped his sister to her feet. "Storm drainage system south of town. Mapped the access points months ago."

She approved of the foresight. "They'll check obvious escape routes. You'll need a diversion."

"What kind of diversion?"

She unshouldered her pack, extracting what she would need and leaving the rest. "I'll draw them north. Away from your exit route."

Thomas stared at her. "That's suicide."

"It's tactics," she corrected. "I move faster alone. Know the territory. Can lose them in the industrial district."

Kate joined them, supporting Ellie. "You don't have to do this."

"Practical choice," she replied. "The girl needs time to evacuate. The antibiotics need time to work."

Simple calculus.

She outlined her plan quickly—create noise to the north, draw the raiders away from the southern drainage access, then circle back east to her original route. Efficient. Logical.

Thomas offered her one of their radios. "Channel three is clear. We can coordinate."

She hesitated, then accepted the device. Temporary tactical advantage. Nothing more.

They separated at the back exit, the family heading south through adjacent buildings while she moved north with purpose. Her pack was lighter now, carrying only essentials. Freedom of movement over comfort. Speed over sustainability.

She reached the commercial district and implemented her plan, using the crowbar to shatter windows in an abandoned department store. The noise echoed through the empty streets—a dinner bell for both infected and raiders.

When the first truck diverted toward the sound, she was already moving to her next position. A car alarm, triggered by smashing the window with her handaxe. More noise. More attention.

The infected came first, drawn by the sounds. She avoided them where possible, eliminated them silently where necessary. The goal was to bring the raiders, not to waste energy on the dead.

It worked. Two of the three trucks converged on the commercial district, raiders fanning out to investigate the disturbances. She observed from the third floor of an office building, counting figures, assessing weapons, calculating angles.

The radio crackled. Thomas's voice, kept professionally low: "Southern exit clear. Moving to checkpoint one."

Good. She clicked the radio once in acknowledgment, then set it aside. No further communication needed. The family would escape. The diversion was working.

Time to extract herself from the situation.

She plotted a route east, away from both the raiders and the family's escape path. Three blocks of careful movement, then she could break into a run once clear of the search area.

She was halfway down the office building stairwell when she heard voices below. Raiders, entering the building. At least three, maybe more.

She froze, evaluating options. The stairwell offered limited mobility. Fighting in confined spaces reduced her advantages. Better to retreat upward, find an alternate exit.

She reversed course silently, ascending to the roof access. Four stories up provided good visibility. She could see the raiders' vehicles below, more men than she had initially calculated. At least twenty, moving with military precision.

Not typical scavengers. Something more organized. More dangerous.

The radio crackled again. "Checkpoint one compromised. Third vehicle cut us off. Need alternate route."

She retrieved the device, processing this new information. The family was pinned down. The raiders had split their forces more effectively than she'd anticipated.

New calculus required.

She keyed the radio. "Location?"

"Market Street pharmacy. Basement level. They're searching the ground floor."

She knew the building. Limited exits. Poor defensive position. If the raiders were thorough, they'd find the family soon.

The logical choice was to continue east. The family's survival odds were low regardless of her intervention. One person against twenty armed raiders was poor tactical math.

Yet she found herself calculating routes to the pharmacy. Assessing weapons. Formulating a plan that prioritized something other than her own survival.

Fifteen minutes later, she approached the pharmacy from the adjacent building, having navigated through interconnected rooftops. The raiders had set up a perimeter, two men guarding the front entrance while others searched inside.

She studied their patterns, noting the radio check-ins. Disciplined. Coordinated. Former military, perhaps.

The alley behind the pharmacy remained unguarded. Oversight or confidence trap? Either way, it was her best option.

She descended a fire escape and moved toward the pharmacy's rear delivery entrance. The door would be locked, possibly alarmed. Direct entry would alert the raiders.

Instead, she examined the building's foundation, finding what she sought near the corner—a storm drain grate leading to the basement level. Likely how the family had entered.

The grate was heavy, but her crowbar provided the necessary leverage. She lowered herself into the darkness below, landing silently on the concrete floor.

The basement was a maze of shelving and storage rooms. She navigated by touch and memory, avoiding debris that might betray her position. Voices filtered down from above—raiders, methodically clearing rooms.

She reached the pharmaceutical storage room where the family should have been hiding.

It was empty.

Blood spattered the floor, a dark trail leading toward the stairs. Fresh. Recent. A smear on the wall at shoulder height. Someone wounded, being dragged.

The radio remained silent. No response to her cautious clicks.

She moved to the base of the stairs, listening. Voices above, triumphant. A woman's sob, quickly silenced. A man—Thomas—pleading.

Too late. The calculus had failed.

She could attempt a rescue. Storm up the stairs, shotgun blazing. Poor odds. Twenty against one. The family already captured, possibly wounded.

Or she could retreat. Live to survive another day. The logical choice.

She hesitated, muscle memory keeping her poised at the base of the stairs. The cold equations balanced in her mind. Their lives against hers. The certainty of her death against the slim possibility of their survival.

A gunshot from above shattered the equation. Then another. And a third.

Execution.

Three lives, extinguished in mathematical sequence. The sound of a body hitting the floor. Thomas's voice, raw with grief, raging against his captors. Then a fourth shot.

Silence.

The calculus resolved itself with brutal finality. No more variables. No more options. The family was gone.

She retreated silently through the storm drain, emerging into the alley as raiders descended to search the basement. Perfect timing, in the wrong direction.

Survival reclaimed its primacy in her calculations. No distractions. No attachments. Just the next step, and the next, and the next.

She circled the building, staying in deep shadow, counting raiders, noting positions. Twenty-three men. Heavily armed. Organized. A significant threat to avoid in the future.

Knowledge was survival.

She was preparing to withdraw when she spotted the lead raider emerging from the pharmacy. Behind him, four men dragged the bodies—Kate, Ellie, James, Thomas. They dumped them unceremoniously in the street, then began checking pockets, removing valuables.

Standard procedure. Harvest the resources. Leave nothing to waste.

The leader gestured toward the trucks. "Load up. We've cleared this sector."

She watched from the shadows as they departed, vehicles rumbling back the way they had come. The bodies remained in the street, discarded resources deemed not worth salvaging.

The antibiotics had been wasted after all.

She waited until the sound of engines faded completely, then approached the bodies. No sentiment. Just calculation. They might have useful supplies.

168

Thomas's eyes stared sightlessly at the sky, his expression frozen in final defiance. His radio was missing. The raiders would monitor that channel now.

She knelt and closed his eyes, a tactically unnecessary gesture that her hands performed without conscious direction.

Ellie still clutched the medication bottle she'd provided. The antibiotics had started working—her skin was cooler than it should have been, given the time elapsed since death.

Another calculation that had failed.

She moved methodically through their pockets, retrieving a folding knife, some matches, a compass. Useful tools. No waste. The dead had no need for resources.

As she searched Kate's body, her fingers encountered a small notebook. A map was tucked inside, hand-drawn, showing river routes and settlement locations. Intelligence. Valuable.

She pocketed the notebook and stood, surveying the scene one final time. Four bodies, arranged like broken dolls in the empty street. Four variables eliminated from the equation.

The raiders would return eventually. Raiders always did. Maybe she would be gone by then. Maybe not.

She shifted her pack, checked her weapons, and turned east—her original heading before the deviation. Back to the plan. Back to the cold calculus of survival.

No regret crossed her face as she moved away from the bodies. No tears marked her passing. Only the mechanical precision of someone who had relearned the fundamental equation of this world: sentiment equaled death.

Alone was survivable. Alone was predictable. Alone was safe.

The horizon stretched before her, empty and unending. She walked toward it with measured steps, each one carrying her further from the brief, failed experiment in human connection.

The next calculation would be simpler. The next decision, colder. The next day, just another variable in the endless equation of survival.

Nothing more.

She walked east, her boots crunching over broken glass and debris, the weight of her pack familiar and grounding. The map she'd taken from Kate's body was tucked securely in her pocket, a small but valuable piece of intelligence. The raiders were gone, their trucks rumbling into the distance, leaving behind only the faint echo of their engines and the bodies of the family she'd tried to save.

But something burned in her chest—a flicker of heat in the cold calculus of her survival. It wasn't regret. It wasn't grief. It was something sharper, angrier. A spark she thought she'd extinguished long ago.

She stopped walking.

The raiders had taken everything from her once before. Not this family, but another. People she'd allowed herself to care about, to fight for. And now, they'd done it again. They'd taken Thomas, Kate, Ellie, and James. They'd executed them like they were nothing. Like they were waste.

Her hand tightened around the grip of her shotgun. The cold calculus in her mind shifted, recalibrating. She could walk away. She should walk away. That was the smart play. The safe play. But the spark in her chest refused to be ignored.

She turned back.

The raiders' camp was easy to find. They weren't trying to hide. Their trucks were parked in a loose circle around an old warehouse, the glow of their fires visible through broken windows. She counted fifteen men outside, laughing and drinking, music blaring from a radio. Their weapons leaned against crates or slung over their shoulders. Inside, there would be more. Maybe another ten. Maybe twenty.

Too many. The logical part of her brain screamed at her to turn around, to disappear into the night. But the spark had grown into a flame, and the flame demanded action.

She didn't charge in. That wasn't her way. Instead, she circled the camp, observing, calculating. She noted the sentries— two on the perimeter, one on the roof of the warehouse. She marked the positions of their weapons, the layout of the trucks, the weak points in their defenses. She waited for the right moment, the right opportunity.

It came when one of the raiders stumbled away from the fire, drunk and careless, to relieve himself in the shadows. She moved like a ghost, her knife finding his throat before he could make a sound. She dragged his body into the darkness, took his rifle, and slung it over her shoulder. One less variable in the equation.

Next, she targeted the sentries. The one on the roof was distracted, staring at the stars. She climbed a nearby tree, steadied her aim, and put a bullet through his skull. The sound was absorbed by the distant revelry and music from the camp, and no one noticed.

The perimeter sentries were harder. She waited until they were on opposite sides of the camp, then took the first one during a rowdy burst of laughter and shouting from the main group—the rifle's crack lost in the cacophony. The second one turned at the sound of the shot, but she was already moving. Her knife found his heart before he could raise the alarm.

Now the camp was blind. She moved to the warehouse, slipping through a gap in the boards. Inside, the raiders were louder, more confident. They hadn't noticed the deaths outside. She counted twelve in the main room, including the leader—a scarred man with a pistol on his hip. He was barking orders, his voice sharp and commanding.

She didn't engage. Not yet. Instead, she sabotaged their vehicles, slashing tires and draining fuel. She set small, controlled fires in the corners of the warehouse, using rags and alcohol from their supplies. The flames spread slowly, giving her time to retreat.

When the first shouts of alarm rang out, she was already outside, watching from the shadows. The raiders scrambled, confused and panicked. Some ran to put out the fires. Others grabbed their weapons, shouting about an attack. The leader tried to restore order, but chaos had taken hold.

She waited until the flames reached the fuel cans she'd placed near the trucks. The explosion was deafening, lighting up the night sky. The raiders screamed, scattering in all directions. She picked them off one by one, her shots precise and deliberate. Those who tried to flee found their vehicles useless, their tires shredded.

The leader was the last to fall. He emerged from the warehouse, coughing and bleeding, his pistol in hand. She stepped into the light, her shotgun leveled at his chest.

"Who are you?" he demanded, his voice hoarse.

She didn't answer. She didn't owe him an explanation. Her finger tightened on the trigger, but he was faster. He dove to the side, rolling behind a crate as her shot tore through the air. He returned fire, forcing her to take cover.

She moved quickly, circling around to flank him. But he was no amateur. He anticipated her movements, his shots forcing her to stay low. She dropped the shotgun and drew her machete, knowing she'd have to get close to finish this.

He emerged from cover, his pistol aimed at her. She threw her knife, the blade spinning through the air and striking his hand. He cursed, dropping the gun, and drew a knife of his own. It was long and serrated, glinting in the firelight.

They circled each other, the heat of the flames pressing in around them. He was bigger, stronger, his movements deliberate and confident. She was faster, her machete held low and ready.

He lunged first, his knife slicing toward her ribs. She sidestepped, bringing the machete down in a swift arc. He blocked it with his forearm, the blade biting into the leather of his jacket but not deep enough to wound. He kicked out, catching her in the stomach and sending her stumbling back.

She recovered quickly, her breath coming in sharp gasps. He pressed the attack, his knife slashing toward her throat. She ducked, feeling the blade graze her shoulder. Pain flared, but she ignored it, driving the machete upward in a brutal strike. He twisted away, but not fast enough—the blade caught him across the side, drawing blood.

He snarled, his movements growing more aggressive. He feinted left, then came in low, his knife slicing across her thigh. She gritted her teeth, the pain sharp and hot, but she didn't falter. She brought the machete down in a heavy overhead strike, forcing him to block. The impact jarred her arms, but she pressed the advantage, driving him back.

He stumbled, his footing unsure on the uneven ground. She saw her opening and took it, sweeping the machete in a wide arc. The blade caught him across the chest, cutting deep. He staggered, his knife slipping from his fingers. She didn't give him a chance to recover. With a final, brutal swing, she brought the machete down on his neck.

He fell to his knees, blood pouring from the wound. His eyes met hers, filled with hate and disbelief, before he collapsed to the ground.

The camp was silent now, the only sound the crackling of the dying fires. She moved through the wreckage, collecting what supplies she could carry—ammunition, food, medical supplies.

The family was still dead. She hadn't saved them. But the raiders who'd killed them were gone. The ones directly responsible, at least.

She stepped outside, the cool night air washing over her. Her wounds ached, but they weren't life-threatening. She'd survive. She always did.

The horizon stretched before her, empty and unending. She adjusted her pack, checked her weapons, and started walking. The flame in her chest had burned out, leaving behind only the cold calculus of survival.

But for the first time in a long time, she felt something else. Not regret. Not grief. Just the faintest flicker of satisfaction.

She had broken her rules. She had made a last-ditch effort. And for once, it had been enough.

Ed Rodriguez

No Horizon: Breaking Chains

The rusted metal door slammed shut with a finality that echoed through the cement-block room. Darkness closed in, broken only by thin strips of light filtering through a narrow grate near the ceiling. She lay motionless on the damp concrete floor, assessing damage: three broken ribs, dislocated shoulder, multiple lacerations. Nothing fatal. Not yet.

Four days ago, she had walked into their trap. The convoy of three vehicles had appeared abandoned on the highway—a perfect scavenging opportunity. Too perfect. Her instincts had screamed warning as she approached the overturned van, but hunger had dulled her edge. She hadn't noticed the fishing line at ankle height until it was too late. The spring-loaded trap had caught her leg, metal teeth tearing through worn boot leather and

179

into flesh. As she'd worked to free herself, they emerged from hiding places within the vehicles.

Eight men. Armed. Organized. The worst kind of survivors.

She had managed to put down three with her shotgun before they overwhelmed her. The last shell had misfired—a rare failure that had cost her everything.

Now she was here, stripped of weapons, gear, dignity. The cell—once a walk-in freezer in what had been a rural steakhouse —held nothing but a bucket in the corner and the faint, metallic smell of old blood. Scratch marks scored the walls to shoulder height. Previous occupants had left their desperation etched into the concrete like primitive cave paintings.

She tested her injured shoulder, wincing as she manually popped the joint back into its socket. Pain lanced down her arm, but mobility returned incrementally. She would need it.

Footsteps approached. The small viewing slot in the door slid open. Eyes peered in, then disappeared. Locks turned. The door opened to admit a man carrying a plastic water bottle and a small foil packet. The leader—they called him Knox—followed, flanked by an armed guard.

"Still alive. Good," Knox said, nudging her with a boot. "Most don't last this long without begging."

She remained silent, eyes tracking movements, calculating distances. The guard stood just beyond optimal striking range, shotgun—her shotgun—held at the ready. Knox crouched down, close enough to smell his unwashed body and the alcohol on his breath.

"We have a system here," he said, gesturing at the room. "You earn your keep, or you feed the biters. Simple economics."

He dropped the foil packet near her hand. Inside was a small piece of jerky and half a protein bar. Bare subsistence.

"Tomorrow you join the others. Rest up." His eyes traveled over her body with deliberate slowness. "You'll need it."

The door closed. Locks engaged. She moved to the corner furthest from the bucket, examining the food packet carefully before consuming its meager contents. The water was stale but uncontaminated. She sipped sparingly, saving half for later.

In the dim light, she inventoried what remained. They had taken her pack, her weapons, her boots, her outer clothing. She still had her tank top, pants, and socks. The hidden ankle sheath that had once held her survival knife was empty, but the sheath itself remained—overlooked in their search.

Most importantly, they had missed the garrote wire sewn into her waistband and the small metal pick hidden in the lining of her pants. Arrogance made men careless. She would make them pay for that carelessness.

She closed her eyes but didn't sleep. Like the predators of the old world, she simply waited.

Morning announced itself with increased light through the grate and the sound of activity in the compound. The door opened, revealing a different guard—younger, nervous. He gestured with a rifle.

"Out. Move."

She complied, limping slightly—partly from her injured leg, partly an affectation to appear weaker than she was. The hallway led to what had once been the restaurant's main dining room. Tables had been pushed against walls to create an open workspace. Four women occupied the room, engaged in various tasks: one cleaning weapons, another sorting through backpacks and equipment—scavenged or stolen—a third mending clothing, and the fourth grinding something with a mortar and pestle.

All wore the hollow-eyed look of the captured. All bore bruises or worse.

The guard shoved her toward the woman sorting equipment. "Help her. Try anything, and Mira gets punished."

The woman cleaning weapons—presumably Mira—didn't look up. Her mechanical movements betrayed long habituation to her circumstances. A faded tattoo on her wrist had been partially obscured by crude scar tissue. Self-inflicted, most likely.

She took her place beside the other woman, who whispered without making eye contact, "I'm Leah. Do what they say. It's easier."

For the next several hours, she sorted, cataloged, and organized the raiders' stolen goods. Her own backpack was among them, emptied of valuables. Her fingers lingered briefly on the familiar fabric before moving on. She memorized the locations of useful items: matches, a multi-tool, medical supplies, ammunition.

Throughout the day, raiders came and went. Some ignored the women entirely. Others made comments or brushed against them deliberately. She kept her head down, watched, listened. By midday, she had counted twelve men total. Four carried sidearms. Three had rifles. The rest relied on melee weapons. Two trucks and a motorcycle were parked outside. Guard rotations changed every four hours.

At dusk, they were herded into a back room—once a kitchen, now a communal cell. Steel counters had been welded to the floor in a square formation. Each woman had a thin blanket on the floor and nothing else.

A fifth woman occupied the space. Older, perhaps fifty, with a gaunt face and dead eyes. Her left arm ended in a poorly healed stump wrapped in dirty bandages.

"That's Clara," Leah whispered, settling onto her blanket. "She's been here longest. Don't stare at the arm."

Clara looked up, eyes focusing briefly. "New one won't last," she muttered. "Too much fight in her eyes."

After the guards locked them in, the women spoke in hushed tones. Their stories emerged in fragments: Mira, captured eight months ago when her group was overrun; Leah, traded by another community for medicine; Elena, the youngest, found hiding in an abandoned school; Clara, who couldn't remember her

184

life before capture. The fifth woman, Dani, said nothing, rocking slightly on her blanket.

"What about you?" Leah asked. "Where were you before?"

She didn't answer. Past and future were irrelevant luxuries. Only the present moment—and how to survive it—mattered.

"They'll put you on sorting duty permanently," Mira said flatly. "You're too dangerous for outside work. Knox can tell."

Clara nodded. "They kill the runners. Samantha tried a few weeks ago. They chained her to the fence post for the biters."

Leah glanced toward the locked door. "There used to be more of us. They trade some to other groups for supplies."

As the others drifted into uneasy sleep, she examined the kitchen. Ventilation ducts too small for escape. Door hinges on the outside. No windows. The only potential weapon was a broken steel ladle that Dani kept hidden under her blanket.

She closed her eyes, listening to the sounds of the compound settling into night routines. Guard conversations outside. Occasional bursts of laughter. The distant moaning of infected drawn to the perimeter by light and sound.

Tomorrow would require strength. She allowed herself exactly four hours of sleep.

Dawn brought Knox himself, accompanied by three guards. He surveyed the women with the clinical detachment of a farmer assessing livestock.

"You," he pointed at her, "and you," Leah, "sorting duty. Elena, perimeter check. Mira, kitchen. Clara, laundry." He glanced at Dani with distaste. "Someone feed her."

The work was the same as the previous day, but now she had purpose behind her movements. Each item categorized was also evaluated for its potential use. Each interaction mapped relationships within the raider group. She noted which men deferred to others, which ones carried keys, which were careless with their weapons.

"Don't bother," Leah whispered, noticing her methodical observation. "Others tried planning escapes. It always ends the same."

She ignored the warning, continuing to sort ammunition into containers. Her hands found a box of shotgun shells—the same caliber as her confiscated weapon. She palmed two shells, slipping them into her waistband when the guard glanced away.

Midday brought a commotion from outside. Two raiders dragged in a struggling man—a lone survivor caught near their territory. Knox interrogated him in full view of the women, asking about other groups, supply caches, functioning infrastructure.

When the man had nothing valuable to offer, Knox nodded to one of his men. The execution was quick, efficient. A resource deemed unworthy of sustaining.

The message was clear: cooperation meant survival. Resistance meant death.

That night, back in the kitchen cell, she began preparing. The wire from her waistband, extracted carefully. The metal pick from her pants lining. The shotgun shells, hidden in the gap between counter and wall. Small advantages, carefully cultivated.

"What's your name?" Elena asked suddenly. "You never said."

She turned, regarding the young woman with steady eyes but remained silent.

"Leave her be," Clara muttered. "Names don't matter anymore."

Leah disagreed. "Names are all we have left."

After the others slept, she worked silently, extracting the primer and powder from one shotgun shell using the metal pick. The crude but effective composition was wrapped carefully in a scrap of fabric torn from the inside of her waistband. She worked through the night, sacrificing rest for preparation.

Three more days passed in the same pattern. Work. Observation. Planning. Each night, she refined her resources, gathering what she needed. A broken piece of spring steel from an abandoned watch. Discarded wire from the sorting room. A small container of flammable lubricant used for the raiders' weapons.

On the fourth night, Knox came for her. Two guards pulled her from the kitchen cell shortly after lockdown. The other women watched with familiar, hollow resignation as she was marched to Knox's quarters—the former manager's office, now converted to private living space.

"I've been patient," Knox said, dismissing the guards with a wave. "Given you time to acclimate. To understand your position." He poured amber liquid from a bottle into a glass, drinking it in one swallow. "Your behavior determines your treatment here. Simple as that."

She stood motionless, eyes cataloging the room's contents. The shotgun—her shotgun—leaned against the desk. Her machete hung on the wall, alongside other trophies. The handaxe lay on a side table. Her possessions, displayed like mounted game.

Knox approached, leaning in with predatory confidence. His eyes lingered on her face as he spoke, voice dropping to a whisper. "Most women come to understand the benefits of cooperation."

His hand reached toward her face. She remained still, waiting for the precise moment.

The door opened unexpectedly. "Boss, we've got movement at the east perimeter," a guard said urgently.

Knox cursed, grabbing the shotgun. "Put her back. We'll continue this conversation later."

The guard marched her back to the kitchen cell. As the lock engaged, shouting erupted from the compound. Flashlight beams were visible through the corridor before the door closed fully. A shot rang out, followed by more shouting.

"Infected breach," Mira said, recognizing the patterns of chaos. "Happens sometimes. They'll contain it."

She moved to the door, examining the lock mechanism with the metal pick. Too complex for simple manipulation. She needed the key, or an alternative.

More gunshots outside. The distinctive boom of her shotgun among them. The compound's attention was divided. It was time.

She retrieved her hidden materials from behind the steel counter. The improvised incendiary device was crude but functional: shotgun powder, lubricant, and the spring steel as an ignition source.

"What are you doing?" Leah whispered, awakened by the movement.

She positioned the device near the door hinges, then motioned the others to move to the far corner, using the steel counters as a barrier.

"Cover your ears," Elena whispered to the others, the first to understand.

The improvised explosive wasn't large, but in the confined space, its effect was sufficient. The blast damaged the upper hinge and frame enough for concentrated force to do the rest. She rammed her shoulder against the weakened door repeatedly until metal screamed and gave way.

The corridor beyond was empty, guards drawn to the perimeter breach. She moved quickly, retrieving a kitchen knife from the preparation area. Not ideal, but better than nothing.

"We have to go now," she said, the first words she had spoken since capture.

Leah hesitated. "They'll hunt us down."

"Not if they're dead," she replied.

Clara and Dani remained frozen, but Mira stood. "I know where they keep the weapons."

Elena joined them. "I can unlock the front gate. I've watched them do it."

Leah, seeing the others move, finally followed. "What's the plan?"

Instead of answering, she led them through the darkened hallway toward the main building. Outside, shouts and gunfire

191

indicated the infected breach was substantial. Good. Chaos created opportunity.

The storeroom was locked but unguarded. Mira pointed to an air vent near the ceiling. "That connects to the next room. I can fit through."

While Mira navigated the vent, she fashioned another incendiary device using the remaining shotgun shell components. The compound's fuel storage was adjacent to the main building— a significant vulnerability she had noted during her observations.

Mira returned with a ring of keys and led them to the armory—a closet reinforced with steel plating. Inside, she found weapons similar to her confiscated ones: a machete, a handaxe, and a crowbar. Her own remained as trophies in Knox's quarters. Her survival knife was missing, but the shotgun would be with Knox.

She distributed weapons to the others. Mira took a baseball bat with nails driven through it. Leah selected a hunting knife and a hammer. Elena, surprisingly, demonstrated familiarity with a compact crossbow.

"I was on the team in high school," she explained quietly.

Outside, the infected breach had been contained, but the commotion had drawn more to the perimeter. Snarls and moans created a constant background noise beneath the shouts of men establishing a defensive line.

"The trucks," she said, pointing to where the vehicles were parked. "We disable two, take the third."

Leah nodded. "What about the men?"

"I'll handle Knox," she replied. "The rest are yours to decide."

They moved as a unit toward the vehicles. Elena peeled off toward the gate controls. Mira and Leah began sabotaging the first truck, slashing tires and fuel lines. She approached the second vehicle, planting the improvised explosive device beneath it, near the fuel tank.

A shout from the main building indicated their escape had been discovered. Flashlight beams cut through the darkness, searching. Gunshots followed. A bullet ricocheted off metal nearby.

She counted five men converging on their position. Knox would be coordinating from the command center—the former restaurant manager's office. She broke from the others, circling behind the building as Mira and Leah provided distraction, drawing fire toward the vehicles.

The rear entrance was unguarded. Inside, she moved silently through familiar hallways. A raider rounded the corner, pistol drawn. The machete took him in the throat before he could shout warning. She caught his weapon as he fell.

The office door was ajar, light spilling into the hallway. Knox's voice carried through, issuing orders via radio to his men outside. Her shotgun lay across his desk, within reach.

She considered options, discarding stealth in favor of directness. The pistol provided the answer. Two shots through the doorway, not aimed to kill but to draw reaction. Knox dove for cover, away from the shotgun. She charged in, machete in one hand, crowbar in the other.

Knox recovered quickly, drawing a handgun from his waistband. Her crowbar knocked it aside. He lunged for the shotgun, fingers closing around the barrel. She brought the machete down, severing his hand at the wrist.

His scream was cut short as the crowbar connected with his jaw. Teeth scattered across the floor like discarded dice. He scrambled backward, leaving a trail of blood, eyes wide with the sudden understanding of prey facing predator.

"Wait," he gurgled through broken teeth and blood. "We can deal—"

The machete ended his negotiation permanently.

She reclaimed her shotgun, checking the action and load. Full magazine. She spotted her empty pack hanging on the wall —another trophy. She grabbed it and quickly filled it with Knox's supplies: ammunition, medical items, water purifiers. The survival knife was in Knox's desk drawer, along with ammunition and keys to the remaining truck.

Outside, chaos had escalated. The improvised explosive had ignited, turning one truck into a fireball that illuminated the compound. The infected, drawn by noise and now fire, pressed against the perimeter fence in growing numbers. Raiders fought a two-front battle against the escaped women and the gathering infected.

Elena had reached the gate controls but was pinned down by gunfire. Mira and Leah had taken cover behind the remaining truck, returning fire with captured weapons. Three raiders were already down, their bodies dark shapes on the concrete.

She circled the building, approaching the raiders from behind. The shotgun made short work of two. The third turned, bringing his rifle to bear. Too slow. The machete opened his abdomen in a spray of viscera that would draw every infected within smelling distance.

Mira saw her emerge from the shadows and nodded in grim acknowledgment. Together they provided covering fire as Leah dashed toward Elena's position. The gate mechanism groaned to life, chain link sliding on metal tracks.

"Go!" she shouted, gesturing toward the functional truck.

As Mira and Elena ran for the vehicle, she approached the fence line. The infected pressed against it, fingers threaded through chain link, mouths working soundlessly. With methodical precision, she used the crowbar to pry open a section of fence opposite from their escape route.

The infected poured in, a flood of rotting flesh and mindless hunger. She retreated toward the truck, where Leah sat behind the wheel, engine running. The remaining raiders found themselves swarmed, their screams adding to the cacophony of moans and snarls.

She climbed into the passenger seat. Behind them, the compound disappeared in flames and chaos. No survivors. No pursuit.

Ten miles down the road, Leah pulled over. The women sat in silence, adrenaline fading, reality settling in.

"What now?" Elena finally asked.

She checked her shotgun, ensuring it was loaded and ready. Her weapons had been cleaned of blood and returned to their proper places in her pack. The survival knife was once again secured in its ankle sheath.

"We go our separate ways," she said, opening the door and stepping out.

Mira leaned forward. "Together we'd have better chances."

She shook her head. "Groups draw attention. Make noise. Slow you down."

"At least tell us your name," Leah said. "So we remember who saved us."

She paused, then looked back at them. "You did," she said quietly.

She shouldered her pack, adjusting the weight distribution with practiced movements. Names were irrelevant. Past identities meaningless. Only survival mattered.

Without another word, she walked away, following the empty highway north. Behind her, the truck's engine started again. Headlights swept across the pavement as the vehicle turned south.

Alone again, she checked her compass and adjusted course. Dawn was approaching, the eastern sky lightening to a dull gray. Her weapons were clean. Her pack was secure. Her body, though battered and bruised, remained functional.

She walked on, alert for movement, attuned to sound. The world had taken everything from her—repeatedly tried to break her—but had failed. She had reclaimed what was hers and left nothing but ashes behind.

In this endless apocalypse, there was no past worth remembering, no future worth planning for. There was only the next step, the next breath, the next kill.

And she was very good at killing.

No Horizon: Blood Arithmetic

Spring brought no mercy to the dead city. Rainwater collected in potholes and craters, breeding mosquitoes that carried who-knew-what between the living and the dead. Vines crept up abandoned buildings, nature reclaiming concrete and steel with silent persistence. The city exhaled decay and damp, a fecund breeding ground for the worst of humanity's remnants—both the walking and the still-breathing varieties.

She moved through the urban landscape with the same methodical precision she applied to everything. Each step calculated, each street crossing preceded by minutes of careful observation. The crumbling downtown district offered both opportunity and danger in equal measure—more buildings meant more potential supplies, but also more blind corners, more places for threats to hide.

Her boots made minimal noise on the wet asphalt as she navigated the maze of abandoned vehicles. The backpack rode comfortably between her shoulder blades, balanced with only essential supplies. The shotgun remained in easy reach across her back, while the machete hung at her hip. The crowbar was secured to the side of her pack, the hand axe tucked into her belt, and the survival knife strapped to her thigh. Five months since winter, and the tools of survival remained unchanged.

A pharmacy stood at the corner of what had once been a busy intersection. Its windows were shattered, the interior dark, but the building itself appeared structurally sound. More importantly, it hadn't been marked with any of the territorial signs used by the various groups of raiders that plagued the city. Worth investigating.

She watched the building for twenty minutes from the shadow of a derelict bus, looking for any sign of movement, any indication of occupation. Nothing visible, but caution remained paramount. Approaching from the side alley would provide better cover and a secondary exit route if needed.

The rear door of the pharmacy had already been forced open, its security bar bent and hanging uselessly. She drew the machete before entering, preferring its silent efficiency to the shotgun's noise in the enclosed space. The interior was thick with dust and the musty smell of water damage, but underneath lingered the antiseptic scent that characterized all medical facilities, however abandoned.

Most of the shelves had been picked clean, but looters were often careless, overlooking valuable supplies in their haste. She worked systematically through the building, checking behind counters, under shelves, inside air vents. The pharmacy tech room yielded a half-empty bottle of iodine solution and a package of sterile gauze. The storage closet contained a forgotten box of latex gloves. All went into her pack.

She was checking behind a fallen display when the sound

of something toppling over outside the rear entrance caught her attention. Moments later came the distinctive shuffle of the undead, not the rapid movements of the infected. At least three, maybe four, entering through the front where the plate glass had been shattered. She crouched lower, listening to their movements, mapping their positions by sound.

The storage room offered a potential exit through a small window, but breaking it would create noise, drawing more attention. The rear door meant potentially encountering whatever had lured the walking dead into the building in the first place. Neither option was optimal.

She moved silently across the pharmacy floor, keeping low behind the counters. The walking dead were spreading out, moving with that horrible aimlessness that belied their true nature as perfect killing machines—unthinking, unfeeling, undistracted by any purpose beyond finding living flesh.

She reached the pharmacy counter and slipped behind it, evaluating options. The shotgun would take them all down but would attract everything within a half-mile radius. The machete was effective but required close proximity to contaminated tissue. This position offered a defensive advantage, with only one direction from which they could approach.

Decision made, she drew the hand axe and waited. The first of the walking dead rounded the counter—once a woman in hospital scrubs, now a gray-skinned husk with exposed ribs visible through its tattered clothing. The axe blade connected with its temple with a wet crunch, and it dropped soundlessly.

The second came from the same direction—smaller, possibly once a teenager. The axe took it in the forehead, the blade sticking momentarily in the skull bone. She wrenched it free just as the third appeared—this one larger, once a man in a security uniform. It lunged forward with unexpected speed, forcing her back against the shelving.

The axe came up too slowly, caught against the counter edge. Its fetid jaws snapped inches from her face, the stench of rot overwhelming. She drove her knee up into its midsection, creating space, then brought the survival knife up under its jaw and into the brain. It collapsed against her, momentarily pinning her beneath its weight.

As she pushed the corpse aside, the sound of breaking glass came from the front of the store. Not random noise— deliberate, purposeful. Living humans, using the walking dead as unwitting scouts. Raiders.

Male voices now, at least two, possibly more: "Check the back room. These freaks were interested in something in here."

"Probably just a rat or some shit."

"Check anyway. And grab anything useful."

She assessed the situation rapidly. Three dead walkers on the floor around her. Raiders approaching. The rear exit now likely blocked by whatever had driven the walking dead inside. The storage room window remained an option, but the breaking glass would give away her position.

The counter provided temporary concealment, but they would find her within minutes. A distraction was needed. She reached into her pack and pulled out the revolver she'd acquired during the winter—the .38 Special with four rounds remaining. Not her preferred option, but necessary now.

She aimed at the ceiling light fixture near the store entrance and fired. The crash of broken glass created the intended chaos. The raiders shouted in confusion: "What the hell?" "Someone's here!" "Spread out!"

In the moment of disorientation, she moved swiftly to the storage room, closing the door behind her. The window was small, but navigable. She used the crowbar to break the glass as quietly as possible, then cleared the frame of remaining shards. Slinging the pack through first, she followed, squeezing through the tight opening.

The alley behind the pharmacy was narrow, lined with dumpsters. She retrieved her pack and moved quickly toward the far end, seeking to put distance between herself and the raiders. Two blocks away, she would circle back to continue the original route. Supplies taken, threats avoided, survival percentages maintained.

She was halfway down the alley when the first shot rang out. A searing pain ripped through her left side, just above the hip, spinning her against the brick wall. The impact knocked the breath from her lungs, but training and instinct took over. She dropped to a crouch, drawing the shotgun in one fluid motion, ignoring the hot wetness spreading across her shirt.

A raider stood at the far end of the alley—male, mid-thirties, hunting rifle raised for a second shot. The shotgun's blast caught him center mass, throwing him backward onto the wet asphalt. The thunderous report echoed between the buildings, but stealth was already compromised.

She chambered another round, scanning for additional threats. None visible, but the shot would draw attention—both human and infected. Escape was now the priority. She pressed her hand against the wound in her side, feeling the warm blood pulsing between her fingers. The bullet had gone through, leaving an entry and exit wound. Not immediately fatal, but potentially so without treatment.

Moving as quickly as the injury allowed, she continued down the alley, cutting through a service entrance into what had once been a restaurant. The kitchen provided momentary shelter as she quickly assessed the damage. The bullet had passed through the flesh above her left hip, missing major organs but tearing through muscle. Blood loss was the primary concern, followed by infection.

She pulled the package of gauze from her pack, pressing several pieces against both wounds, then used duct tape to secure them in place—a temporary measure until proper treatment could be administered. The iodine would be needed once she found secure shelter. For now, stopping the bleeding took priority.

The restaurant connected to a small shopping arcade, providing covered movement through several blocks. She progressed with one hand on the shotgun, the other pressed against her side, leaving a trail of blood droplets despite her best efforts. Each movement sent fresh waves of pain through her body, but pain was merely information—useful for assessment, irrelevant to decision-making.

Two infected rushed her from a darkened storefront—once-humans in the final stages of the disease, moving with that frenzied speed that made them more dangerous than the walking dead. The shotgun's report filled the enclosed space as she took down the first. The second closed the distance before she could chamber another round, forcing her to drive the machete up through its jaw and into its brain. The exertion tore at her wound, fresh blood soaking through the gauze.

The arcade exit led to a small courtyard surrounded by office buildings. Too exposed. She diverted to a service stairwell, climbing despite the protests of her injured body. Height provided defensive advantages, and the upper floors of most buildings remained unexplored by casual raiders. The third floor of the office building offered temporary security—high enough to be overlooked, low enough to escape if necessary.

Inside a former insurance office, she barricaded the door

with a desk, then collapsed into an office chair, her body finally acknowledging the trauma it had sustained. The adrenaline was fading, allowing the full measure of pain to register. Sweat beaded on her forehead as she carefully removed her pack and outer layers.

The makeshift bandages were soaked through with blood. Not good. She peeled them away carefully, examining the wounds with clinical detachment. The entry wound was a neat hole, but the exit wound was ragged, leaving torn flesh and exposed muscle. Both seeped blood steadily.

First priorities: sterilize, close, cover. She uncapped the iodine bottle and, after a moment of mental preparation, poured it directly into both wounds. The burning sensation was excruciating, forcing a sharp gasp through clenched teeth. Her body tensed, hands gripping the edges of the chair as the antiseptic did its work.

Closing the wounds presented a greater challenge. Proper medical sutures would be ideal, but weren't available. She reached into her pack and removed the dental floss she'd scavenged months ago. Not sterile, but treated with the remaining iodine, it would serve. The survival knife, heated over a small alcohol flame, provided a cutting edge.

The needle was the difficult part. She searched the office methodically, finding a sewing kit in a secretary's desk drawer. The needle was small, designed for fabric rather than flesh, but it would have to do. She sterilized it with the flame, then threaded it with the treated floss.

Suturing one's own wound required a particular kind of detachment. She approached it methodically, starting with the exit wound. Each puncture of the needle through flesh brought fresh waves of pain, but she worked steadily, drawing the torn edges together with small, even stitches. The entry wound was simpler, requiring fewer sutures.

With both wounds closed, she applied the remaining gauze, securing it with more duct tape. The impromptu surgery had cost her nearly an hour of daylight, and her body was showing signs of shock—clammy skin, accelerated heart rate, lightheadedness. Rest was necessary, but extended vulnerability was not an option.

She forced herself to drink water, then chewed a strip of jerky from her rations. Calories and hydration would help combat shock. An antibiotic tablet—part of her carefully conserved medical supplies—would help fight potential infection. The office couch would provide adequate rest without the danger of deep sleep.

As dusk approached, she set up minimal security—an overturned filing cabinet near the door that would create noise if disturbed, the shotgun within immediate reach. Three hours of rest, no more. The city became more dangerous after dark, when both the infected and human raiders grew bolder.

Sleep came in fits, interrupted by pain and the constant alertness that had kept her alive this long. Dreams, when they came, were fragmented images of blood on snow, of hands performing surgeries, of quiet rooms filled with silent screams.

In one recurring moment, a child's drawing on the office wall swam into focus – a crude crayon family, smiling beneath a yellow sun. Her fingertips hovered near it, not quite touching. The motion triggered a calculation she usually suppressed – a cost-benefit analysis of attachment, memory, sentiment. All luxuries in this new world, expenses that drained limited cognitive resources, distractions that could prove fatal.

Yet the equation persisted. Her eyes traced the smallest stick figure in the drawing, and her mind produced a grim assessment. Children rarely survived this world. Their size, their noise, their inability to process danger correctly – all liabilities in pure survival terms. She'd seen so few of them in recent months, each sighting rarer than the last.

She closed her eyes, forcing the calculation away. Something inside her – not the bullet wound, but elsewhere, deeper – throbbed with a different kind of pain. The quantifiable self she had constructed was efficient, logical, functional. It kept her alive in a world that wanted her dead. But in moments of weakness, like now, with blood seeping through improvised stitches and fever beginning to cloud her thoughts, the old calculations sometimes surfaced – the ones involving worth and meaning. The ones asking what survival was for.

She pressed her fingers against the bullet wound, using physical pain to override these dangerous thoughts. Pain was information. Information could be processed, categorized, acted upon. These other sensations – regret, longing, doubt – were not actionable data. They were system errors, corrupted files to be quarantined and deleted.

She woke precisely three hours later, immediately alert despite the throbbing pain in her side.

The wound needed regular checking. She peeled back the gauze carefully, examining her handiwork in the fading light. The stitches held, though the surrounding skin was red and hot to the touch—early signs of infection. The remaining iodine went directly onto the wounds again, followed by fresh gauze.

Moving hurt, but remaining stationary meant death. She

213

gathered her supplies, redistributing the weight in her pack to avoid pressure on the injured side. Standing brought a wave of dizziness that she pushed through with practiced determination. Time to move again.

The office building offered one significant advantage—interconnected rooftops that could provide a path across several blocks without street-level exposure. She made her way to the roof access, each step measured against the pain it produced.

The spring evening was cool, the city spread out before her like a decaying chessboard. From this height, she could see movement in the streets—clusters of walking dead, drawn by the earlier gunshots, and the occasional flashlight beam indicating human activity. None had tracked her to this location yet.

She crossed to the adjacent rooftop via a maintenance walkway, her pace slower than usual but deliberate. The destination remained clear in her mind—a hospital three blocks east. Not for the obvious medical supplies, which would have been thoroughly looted, but for something commonly

214

overlooked: the mechanical rooms housing backup generators.

Such areas were typically secure, isolated, and contained maintenance cots for workers on extended shifts. More importantly, they often contained first aid supplies designed for industrial accidents—the kind that included stronger antibiotics and proper wound care materials.

The second rooftop led to a fire escape that she descended carefully, each movement pulling at her stitches. The alley below was clear for the moment, though sounds of infected could be heard from the adjacent street. She kept to the shadows, moving with as much stealth as her injury permitted.

Two blocks passed without incident, but the third presented a complication. A group of raiders had established a checkpoint in front of the hospital, complete with barricades and lookouts. Their presence suggested the building might still contain valuable supplies, but also made it inaccessible by conventional means.

She observed them from the shelter of an abandoned

ambulance. Five visible, likely more inside. Armed with a mixture of firearms and melee weapons. Organized enough to establish a perimeter, which indicated leadership and planning—the most dangerous kind of survivor group.

A direct confrontation was not viable in her current condition. Alternative entry points needed to be identified. She circled the hospital complex, keeping to cover, noting possible access routes. The loading dock at the rear was less heavily guarded—only one lookout, positioned on the roof rather than at ground level. The dock itself was littered with the corpses of infected that had been cleared from the area—evidence of regular defense but also potential cover.

As she assessed the scene, she noticed something unexpected – partially concealed between two corpses lay a small portable oxygen tank. Medical-grade, with intact regulator and gauge showing half-full. Someone must have dropped it during a retreat, the chaos of combat leaving this valuable resource behind. In her current state, with fever threatening and blood loss already affecting her cognitive function, having supplemental oxygen could mean the difference between clarity and confusion, between precision and error. Between survival and death.

She waited until the lookout's attention was directed elsewhere, then moved quickly across the open space to the loading dock, concealing herself among the piled corpses. The stench was overwhelming, but the dead provided excellent camouflage—the living avoided them instinctively, while the infected overlooked anything that already smelled of death.

She reached for the oxygen tank, securing it carefully to her pack. The added weight strained her injured side, but the potential benefit outweighed the immediate cost. Every tool had its purpose; every resource its time. Her fingers moved automatically to verify the regulator's seal, checking the pressure gauge – still half full. Sufficient.

The loading dock door was secured with a chain and padlock, but the adjacent window had been broken. She slipped through, finding herself in a dark corridor that smelled of mold and antiseptic. The hospital interior was littered with debris—abandoned gurneys, scattered medical equipment, occasional corpses in various states of decay. She moved through it silently, following the emergency signage toward the building's core.

The mechanical rooms would be in the basement or sub-basement, away from patient areas. She located a service stairwell and began her descent, the pain in her side now a constant companion. The loss of blood had weakened her more than she'd initially calculated, requiring additional caution with each step.

The basement level was flooded with several inches of stagnant water, the result of months without maintenance to the drainage systems. She waded through it carefully, testing each step for submerged hazards. The mechanical room was identified by a simple sign: "Generator Room - Authorized Personnel Only."

The door was locked, but yielded to the crowbar with minimal effort. Inside, the space was dry, windowless, and—most importantly—secure. Heavy equipment filled most of the room, with a small workspace containing a cot, desk, and wall-mounted first aid kit. Perfect.

She secured the door behind her, propping a metal stool against the handle as a simple alarm system. The generator would provide an additional advantage—if operational, it could power essential medical equipment. She examined it briefly, noting that it was a diesel model with a half-full tank gauge. Potential emergency power if absolutely necessary, though the noise would attract unwanted attention.

The first aid kit exceeded expectations—proper suture materials, antibiotic ointment, sterile bandages, and, most valuable of all, a sealed package of injectable antibiotics with unused syringes. Hospital-grade supplies meant for treating maintenance workers injured on duty.

She removed her blood-stained clothing and examined the wounds again. The improvised stitches had held, but the surrounding skin showed more pronounced signs of infection—

red streaks beginning to radiate outward, the flesh hot and swollen. The wound needed to be properly cleaned, re-sutured, and treated with stronger antibiotics than she currently had in her system.

Working methodically, she cleaned both wounds thoroughly with antiseptic wipes from the kit. The process was painful but necessary. She removed her amateur stitches with the knife tip, applied antibiotic ointment liberally to both wounds, then re-closed them with proper medical sutures—smaller, neater, and less likely to leave significant scarring.

The injectable antibiotics presented a different challenge. She'd observed enough medical procedures to understand the basics, but self-administration required precision. Following the printed instructions, she prepared a syringe, located a vein in her arm, and injected the antibiotic with steady hands despite the pain and fatigue.

With the immediate medical needs addressed, she turned her attention to the oxygen tank. Setting up the mask and regulator, she allowed herself five minutes of supplemental oxygen – not enough to deplete the tank significantly, but sufficient to improve her blood-oxygen levels and counteract the effects of blood loss. As the pure oxygen filled her lungs, her mind cleared fractionally, the calculations becoming more precise, the variables more distinct.

Fresh bandages completed the treatment. She changed into the spare shirt from her pack—the last clean one—and drank deeply from her water supply. The medical exertion had exhausted her already weakened body, but security considerations remained paramount. She did a final check of the room's perimeter, ensuring all potential access points were covered.

The cot provided better rest than she'd had in weeks. Six hours this time, a calculated risk balanced against the need for recovery. She arranged her weapons within immediate reach—the shotgun beside the cot, the knife under the pillow, the revolver on the small table next to her. Sleep came quickly, deeper than before but still alert to any change in the environment.

During these hours of forced recovery, her mind drifted back to the oxygen tank – a random find that might save her life. The universe rarely offered such gifts. Most "luck" was actually careful preparation meeting opportunity, yet occasionally pure chance intervened. Finding the tank wasn't luck though – it was observation, assessment, risk calculation. Skills she had honed to mechanical precision.

As the fever ebbed and flowed, her thoughts became less ordered, memories and scenarios blurring together. She found herself calculating strange equations – measuring the precise weight of a human life against canisters of fuel, bottles of antibiotics, rounds of ammunition. The familiar arithmetic of survival, but with unfamiliar variables interrupting the clean lines of her logic.

What was the mathematical value of continuing? Each day survived merely led to another day requiring survival. The equation stretched toward infinity without resolution. In her work before, there had always been endpoints, objectives, measurable outcomes. Now existence had become circular, a loop of calculations without conclusion.

Her ruthless efficiency kept her body alive, but to what purpose? The question itself was dangerous – a recursive function that consumed processing power better allocated elsewhere. Yet in her weakened state, the inquiry persisted. There had been a time when her calculations included variables beyond immediate survival – future planning, community benefit, knowledge preservation. Larger equations that made the daily arithmetic of staying alive serve a greater function.

As she drifted in and out of consciousness, fever dreams mixing with fragmented memories, she realized these broader calculations weren't luxuries or distractions but essential components of true survival. Her methodical efficiency kept her body functioning, but without these other equations – the ones that reached beyond immediate self-preservation – what exactly was she preserving?

She woke with this realization still lingering at the edges

of her consciousness, filing it away like any other useful data point. The fever had broken during her rest, her body responding to the professional-grade antibiotics. The system was functioning again, optimized and operational.

The room had served its purpose as a temporary shelter and medical station. Now it was time to move on before the raiders expanded their search deeper into the building.

She retraced her path to the loading dock, moving more easily than the previous day but still cautious of the injury. The raiders' checkpoint remained in place, but their attention was diverted by a new development—a small herd of infected approaching from the east, drawn by unknown stimuli.

The diversion provided an opportunity. As the raiders engaged the infected, she slipped away from the hospital complex, keeping to the shadows of adjacent buildings. By the time the skirmish ended, she would be blocks away, her presence unknown, her passage unmarked.

The city continued its slow decay around her, indifferent

to the struggle of its remaining inhabitants. Spring rain began to fall, washing away blood and footprints alike. She adjusted her jacket to better shield her injury and continued her methodical progress through the urban wilderness.

Another day survived. Another wound endured. The calculations remained unchanged—assess, decide, execute, survive. There was no victory in this world, only continued existence. No horizon beyond the next shelter, the next supply cache, the next threat eliminated.

She moved through the rain with determined steps, already mapping the next location, the next objective. The injury would heal, becoming just another scar on a body that served as its own historical record of survival. Pain was temporary. Weakness was not an option.

The dead city breathed around her—a living entity composed of countless threats, opportunities, and neutral factors, all to be calculated and incorporated into the endless equation of survival. She was merely one variable in this new world's mathematics, but she had no intention of being factored out. And perhaps, in the precisely balanced arithmetic of her existence, survival itself wasn't the final sum but merely part of a more complex calculation.

No Horizon: Dead Ends

The low growl emerged from somewhere behind the abandoned gas station. She froze, one foot poised mid-step, her weight distributed to minimize sound. A second growl joined the first, then a third.

Three was manageable. Five would be pushing it.

She slowly lowered her boot to the pavement, careful to avoid the broken glass scattered across the cracked surface. Her right hand drifted to the machete sheathed at her hip while her left adjusted the shotgun slung across her back. Not yet. The shotgun was a last resort—too loud, too wasteful. Each shell was precious currency in this dead world.

227

A feral dog rounded the corner of the gas station, ribs visible beneath matted fur. Not infected, just hungry. Dangerous all the same. The animal bared yellowed teeth, saliva dripping from its jaws. Two more followed, then another three. Six total. Too many.

She took a step back, maintaining eye contact with what appeared to be the alpha—a large German Shepherd mix with a torn ear and scarred muzzle. The pack spread out in a semi-circle, instinctively cutting off escape routes. These weren't mindless infected or shambling dead. These were hunters, working as a unit.

Behind her stood an overturned semi-truck. To her right, a drainage ditch choked with debris. Left, the open road leading back to the town she'd just scavenged. Forward, through the pack, lay her intended path—an access road that, according to her map, led to a research facility. Potential supplies, potential shelter.

The alpha lunged forward in a feint. She didn't flinch. It backed up, reassessing. Smart. The two smaller dogs to her right inched closer. Coordinated attack imminent.

She'd been tracking this pack for two days, though they likely believed they were tracking her. Feral dogs had claimed this territory, picking off infected stragglers and unwary survivors alike. She'd observed their hunting patterns—they preferred to chase fleeing prey into an ambush point where half the pack would be waiting.

When the attack came, it was swift. The alpha and two others charged from the front while the remaining three circled to her flanks. She drew the machete in one fluid motion, simultaneously backing toward the overturned semi. The first dog —a malnourished pit bull—leapt for her arm. The machete caught it mid-air, opening its throat in a clean arc. No time to watch it fall.

The second attacker, a rangy mutt with one eye, dove for her legs. She pivoted, driving her boot into its skull with a sickening crack. The remaining dogs hesitated, unused to prey that fought back effectively.

She used the moment to slip beneath the semi-trailer, dragging her pack after her. The confined space wasn't ideal, but it neutralized their numerical advantage. One dog tried to follow, snapping at her boots. She kicked out, connecting with its snout. It yelped and retreated.

The pack circled the trailer, occasionally darting in only to be met with the machete's edge. Blood soaked into the asphalt beneath her. Eventually, the animals withdrew to a safe distance, unwilling to sustain more casualties but equally unwilling to abandon potential food.

A standoff.

She shifted position, taking inventory of her immediate options. The semi's undercarriage offered temporary shelter but no exit strategy. The pack had settled into a loose perimeter, with the alpha maintaining a watchful position directly opposite her hiding spot. Patient predators could wait for hours. She couldn't.

From her pack, she retrieved an emergency flare. Not her preferred solution, but necessity dictated terms. She struck the flare against the ignition strip. It burst to life with a hiss and a flood of harsh red light. The dogs backed away, wary of the fire and smoke.

She rolled the flare out from beneath the trailer, away from her intended path. Two of the dogs fled immediately. The others, including the alpha, retreated to a cautious distance. Not enough.

Her hand found the shotgun. One shell would scatter them, but would also announce her presence to everything within a half-mile radius. The infected were drawn to noise. The dead shambled toward it. Human survivors investigated it.

Risk assessment: manageable.

She pulled the shotgun forward, chamber already loaded. One deep breath, then she slid out from the opposite side of the trailer from where she'd tossed the flare. The alpha spotted her immediately, ears flattening against its skull as it charged.

The shotgun's report echoed across the empty landscape. The alpha's chest disappeared in a spray of red. The remaining dogs scattered into the surrounding brush, their survival instincts overriding their hunger.

She was moving before the echo faded, heading toward the access road at a steady jog. No running—running was for prey. But no lingering either. The clock was ticking. Anything within earshot would be converging on this position.

The access road curved through sparse woodland, eventually revealing a chain-link fence topped with barbed wire. Beyond it stood a complex of low buildings with the weathered look of government construction. "Lakeside Research Station" read the faded sign beside the gate. The fence had been breached in several places, the gate itself hanging from a single hinge.

Fresh tracks in the mud—both human boots and the distinctive shuffling drag of the dead. Recent, within the last day. She crouched, examining the patterns. Three humans, moving with purpose toward the facility. At least a dozen dead, following sometime after.

She moved through the gap where the gate had once been, machete now in hand. The shotgun remained accessible, but silence was preferable. The facility's parking lot contained abandoned vehicles, their windows smashed, several showing the dark brown stains of old violence.

A tactical sweep of the exterior revealed multiple entry points. The main entrance doors stood propped open with a concrete block. Rookie mistake. She opted instead for a service entrance on the building's western face, picking the simple lock with practiced efficiency.

The service corridor was dark and undisturbed. She produced a small flashlight from her vest pocket, holding it alongside the machete in her left hand. The beam revealed dusty floors with only a few scattered footprints—most traffic had gone through the main entrance. Smart. She'd avoid whatever attracted that traffic.

Room by room, she cleared the western wing. Offices, storage rooms, janitor's closets. She collected useful items methodically: half a box of nitrile gloves, a first-aid kit with unexpired antiseptic, battery cells, duct tape. Each item went into specific compartments in her pack, organized for quick access.

A floor plan mounted beside a fire extinguisher provided orientation. The facility was arranged in four wings around a central atrium. The western wing contained administrative offices. North held laboratories. East contained long-term residential quarters. South housed utilities and storage.

She made her way toward the northern wing, moving silently despite the weight of her pack and weapons. A crash from somewhere ahead stopped her mid-step. Voices followed— human voices, stressed and urgent.

"It's locked! We need the keycard!"

"Check his pockets! Hurry!"

She flattened against the wall, extinguishing her light. The voices came from the central atrium. Male, young, panicked. The survivors whose tracks she'd spotted outside.

"They're coming! Get the door open!"

A chorus of moans provided context to their panic. The dead had followed them inside, probably through the propped-open main entrance. Amateur mistake.

She changed course, heading deeper into the administrative wing to circumvent the atrium entirely. The floor plan had shown connecting corridors between all wings. No need to involve herself in someone else's poor planning.

The connecting door to the northern wing required a keycard. She retrieved her crowbar, wedging it into the door frame near the electronic lock. Applying steady pressure, she felt the frame begin to give. A sharp crack announced her success as the striker plate tore free from the wall.

Beyond lay darkness and the distinctive smell of scientific laboratories—chemicals, cleaning agents, and beneath it all, the sweet-sour stench of decay.

Her flashlight revealed an abandoned research space. Computer terminals sat dark and silent. Papers littered the floor, some stained with substances best left unidentified. Tables held sophisticated equipment now gathering dust. One wall featured a sealed containment chamber with thick glass windows, its interior dark.

More interesting were the whiteboards still covered in fading marker. Complex formulas, charts, and hastily scrawled notes documented the final days of the facility's operation. She approached, studying the information methodically.

The earliest dates showed organized research notes—viral replication rates, cellular degradation patterns, protein markers. Later entries became increasingly disjointed:

"Containment breach in Section 4. Three researchers exposed."

"Mechanism unknown. Traditional antivirals ineffective."

"Mutation rate accelerating. Original assumptions invalid."

"Reanimation confirmed 4.3 hours post-mortem. Central nervous system activity detected despite clinical death."

The final entry, written in jagged, hurried script: "No cure possible. Fundamental structure defies conventional approaches. God help us all."

She stared at those words for a long moment, her expression unchanged. Then she turned away, continuing her search through the laboratories.

A locked cabinet yielded its contents to her crowbar: antibiotics, analgesics, suture kits. Practical medicine, no miracles. She transferred them to her pack methodically, mentally cataloging each item.

The screams from the atrium had stopped. Either the survivors had escaped or, more likely, they hadn't. The moaning of the dead continued, but seemed to be moving away from her position. Good.

She found the secure storage room at the back of the laboratory wing. Its heavy door stood partially open, the electronic lock disabled by a previous visitor. Inside, refrigeration units designed to preserve biological samples sat dark and useless. A faint odor of putrefaction suggested their contents had long since spoiled.

One wall was dominated by a large display screen. A generator hummed softly beneath it—someone had restored emergency power to this section. The screen glowed with a paused video file. Beside it, a body slumped in a chair, a neat hole in its temple and a pistol still clutched in its stiffened hand. The white lab coat bore a name tag: "Dr. Allen Mercer, Lead Virologist."

She studied the body clinically. No signs of infection or reanimation. A choice, then. Perhaps after viewing whatever was on the screen.

She pressed play.

A haggard version of the dead man appeared on screen, his eyes sunken with exhaustion and something deeper—despair.

"This is Dr. Allen Mercer, recording what will likely be the final research update from Lakeside Station," the recording began. "It's been seventeen days since initial containment failure. Twelve days since external communications went dark. Eight days since military personnel abandoned their posts."

The man rubbed his eyes, continuing in a clinical tone that belied the content of his words.

"Our findings are conclusive and devastating. The pathogen combines aspects never before observed in nature— viral transmission vectors with prion-like protein misfolding capabilities. Initial infection presents as extreme aggression and loss of higher brain function. Upon host death, the pathogen triggers a secondary phase, reactivating basic motor functions and predatory instincts while continuing to spread."

The doctor's voice cracked slightly.

"We've exhausted every conventional treatment approach. The pathogen adapts too quickly. Its structure is too alien. Even if we had unlimited resources and time... there's simply no medical solution to be found. Not with current science."

He leaned toward the camera, his professional facade finally crumbling.

"If anyone finds this... I'm sorry. We tried. God, we tried. But there's no way back from this. No cure. No vaccine. No herd immunity. Just... adaptation. Those who can survive in this new world will. Those who can't..."

The doctor glanced down at the pistol visible on his desk.

"This is Dr. Allen Mercer, Lakeside Research Station. This will be my final report."

The screen went black.

She reached forward and ejected the storage drive containing the video, examining it briefly before pocketing it. Not because the information was new—she'd suspected as much for months. But confirmation had value. Knowledge, even hopeless knowledge, was power.

A commotion in the hallway pulled her attention away from the screen. The distinct shuffle-thump of dead feet. Multiple sets. The survivors from earlier, perhaps, now transformed and hunting.

She moved to the door, peering through the narrow opening. Three dead shuffled past, their clothes bearing the distinctive tears of infected attacks. Not the survivors from the atrium—lab coats suggested former staff. They moved away from her position, drawn by some sound or movement elsewhere in the facility.

After they passed, she slipped out, heading toward the eastern residential wing. Night would fall soon. The facility, despite its grim findings, offered shelter more secure than most. She would rest, regroup, then continue her journey tomorrow.

The residential wing was surprisingly intact. She selected a corner room on the second floor with windows facing both east and south—optimal visibility and two potential escape routes via adjacent rooftops. The door was solid, the lock functional. The room's previous occupant had left behind few personal effects:

some clothes she could repurpose as rags, scientific journals now useful only as fire starter, a half-empty bottle of whiskey.

She set up her security measures methodically. Tripwire near the door connected to a cluster of empty food cans. Window blind adjusted to allow monitoring of the grounds below. Furniture positioned to provide cover if needed. Every action economical, practiced, automatic.

With security established, she allowed herself a moment to process what she'd learned. The doctor's confirmation matched her own observations over months of survival. The world wasn't sick. It wasn't broken. It was transformed. Permanently.

She uncapped the whiskey bottle, taking a measured sip. Not for comfort or escape—she allowed herself no such luxuries. It was simply calories and chemical relief for tired muscles. Still, the burn as it went down seemed appropriate to the moment.

From her pack, she retrieved a worn leather journal and a pencil. She opened to a page filled with neat, precise handwriting, and added a new entry:

"Lakeside Research Station confirms no cure possible. Conventional medicine useless against pathogen. Adaptation only option."

She paused, pencil hovering over the page. Then added: "Continue north. Locate winter shelter before first snow."

The task complete, she returned the journal to its place and began preparing a small meal from her rations. No fire—cold food was safer than the risk of smoke or light. She ate methodically, efficiently, her mind already planning tomorrow's route.

Outside, darkness fell. In the distance, the howl of a lone dog—perhaps the last of the pack she'd encountered—echoed across the dead landscape. Closer, the occasional moan or shuffling footstep revealed the facility's current inhabitants going about their endless, mindless search.

She finished her meal and positioned herself near the window, shotgun across her lap. Four hours of rest, then four hours of watch, then movement at first light. The routine never changed because the routine kept her alive.

The world had ended. Medicine had failed. Hope, at least as people once understood it, was extinct. These were simply facts, neither tragic nor heartbreaking. They were reality, and reality was something to be faced, assessed, and navigated.

She had no illusions about salvation, no fantasies of restoration. The horizon offered nothing but more of the same—danger, scarcity, vigilance. But she would meet that horizon step by measured step, weapon by tested weapon, day by calculated day.

Not because she believed things would improve.

But because she refused to do anything else.

No Horizon: Winter's Child

The muffled sounds of shuffling and scratching echoed through the abandoned two-story colonial. She paused at the threshold, shotgun raised, listening. Snow drifted in through the shattered kitchen window, collecting in small dunes across the linoleum floor. Her breath clouded before her face as she stepped inside, boots crunching on broken glass and plaster dust.

Three days since the last snowfall, and the house showed no tracks. Good. She'd cleared four homes in this neighborhood already—slim pickings, but enough to justify the risk. This was the last house on the street and seemed untouched since whatever exodus or extinction had emptied it.

The scratching sound came again, upstairs. Rhythmic, persistent. Not wind.

She eased the kitchen drawers open with her crowbar. Empty. The pantry yielded a forgotten can of peaches and a jar of peanut butter with a third left. She slipped them into her pack, calculating the calories against the effort expended. Still worth it.

The scratching intensified, accompanied by a low moan that carried down the stairwell. The undead, not the infected. The infected screamed; the undead moaned. Different threats, different tactics.

Securing the first floor took less than three minutes. Habit kept her thorough despite the promise of what lurked above. The living room held nothing of value; the dining room offered three tealight candles and a box of matches with four left. She pocketed them without breaking stride.

At the foot of the stairs, she swapped the shotgun for the machete. The undead were slow. In tight spaces, silence trumped firepower. Ammunition was finite; opportunities for stealth were situational.

As she ascended, the steps creaked beneath her weight. The scratching stopped. Then resumed with renewed vigor. The sound came from behind a door at the end of the upstairs hallway. She approached methodically, checking each bedroom and bathroom on her way. A linen closet yielded an unopened first-aid kit—uncommon fortune.

When she reached the door, she understood. Two of them —one male, one female—both in advanced stages of decay, pawing at a bedroom door. The smell hit her first: the sweet-rot stench of necrosis. The male wore the remnants of a flannel shirt, now dark with old blood. The female's flowered housedress hung in tatters.

The door they clawed at was different from the others: reinforced with a chair wedged under the handle. Someone had tried to secure it from the outside.

She advanced silently, machete raised. The male turned first, jaw hanging at an unnatural angle, one eye milky and vacant, the other missing entirely. Easy targets, spaced perfectly for sequential elimination.

The female lunged unexpectedly—faster than the undead should move. She sidestepped but her boot slipped on a patch of frozen condensation. Her elbow struck the wall, sending a ceramic picture frame crashing to the floor.

The male closed in as she regained her balance. She swung the machete, aiming for the neck, but the blade caught on the door frame, deflecting into the shoulder instead. Useless. The creature pressed forward, putrid hands grasping.

She abandoned the stuck blade, drawing her survival knife. Too close now for proper leverage. The female grabbed her pack from behind, pulling her off-balance. Rookie mistake. She'd underestimated their coordination, treated them like standard shamblers when they clearly retained some rudimentary pack behavior.

The knife plunged into the male's eye socket, but not deep enough. He kept coming. Her back hit the wall. The female's teeth snapped inches from her neck. She reached for the handaxe on her belt.

A deafening crack echoed through the hallway. The male's head exploded in a spray of blackened matter. The female turned toward the sound. A second shot tore through its temple, dropping it instantly.

She whirled toward the shooter, knife ready.

The bedroom door had opened a crack. Through it, the barrel of a small-caliber pistol and a single blue eye.

"Are you bit?" A child's voice, unwavering.

She shook her head once.

The door opened wider. A girl stood there, perhaps ten or eleven years old, hollow-cheeked but steady on her feet. The pistol—a .22 target shooter—remained pointed center mass.

"You have to get the brain," the girl said flatly. "Every time."

The girl's eyes drifted to the bodies, lingering for a moment too long. Recognition. The man's flannel shirt. The woman's flowered dress. Parents, then. Recently turned, judging by their mobility. The chair under the doorknob—someone had tried to protect the child by locking her in. Or perhaps protect others from what they knew she would become.

A crash downstairs broke the moment. Glass shattering. The unmistakable hungry keening of the infected. Not one. Many.

"They follow noise," the girl whispered, unnecessarily.

She retrieved her machete, wiping the blade on the carpet. Nine, maybe twelve infected, judging by the sounds. Too many for close quarters. They'd need to move.

The window at the end of the hall overlooked the backyard. Twenty-foot drop to frozen ground. Not an option with a child.

She gestured toward the stairs with her blade, then held up a hand. Wait. From her pack, she withdrew a road flare. The bright crimson tube would draw them, create a diversion.

The infected reached the bottom of the stairs as she struck the flare to life. The harsh chemical smell filled the hallway as bright red light painted the walls. She hurled it into the bathroom at the opposite end of the hall, then pulled the door nearly closed.

The infected swarmed up the stairs—faster than the undead, more reckless. Driven by rage rather than hunger. The first reached the landing, foam flecking its lips and chin. Blood vessels had burst in its eyes, giving them a hellish red appearance. It spotted the light under the bathroom door and charged.

"Back," she mouthed to the girl, gesturing toward the bedroom. The girl nodded, understanding immediately. Smart kid.

As the infected crowded the bathroom door, tearing at it and each other in their frenzy, she grabbed the girl's hand and pulled her toward the stairs. The first one noticed them too late. She drove her knife through its ear canal, into the brain. It dropped without a sound.

The shotgun came up next. Two shells, fired in rapid succession, cleared the stairwell. The sound would bring more, but it bought precious seconds. They descended amid the twitching bodies of the fallen infected. Three shells left. She'd have to make them count.

The kitchen door offered the clearest exit. More infected spilled through the front entrance as they reached the bottom of the stairs. She shoved the girl ahead, through the kitchen, covering their retreat with the shotgun's final rounds.

Outside, the winter air bit at exposed skin. Daylight was fading fast. The girl wore only a sweater and jeans, inadequate for the temperature. She shed her outer layer—a weatherproof shell—and draped it over the child's shoulders without breaking stride. Practicality, not kindness. Hypothermia would slow them both.

They made it a few blocks before the girl spoke again.

"Where are we going?"

North, toward the abandoned strip mall where a group of traders had established a semi-permanent camp. Two days' journey in good weather. Longer in snow. She pointed.

"The mall?" the girl asked. "My dad said those people can't be trusted."

Her dad was now a headless corpse in a hallway. His opinions had expired with him. She kept moving.

Night fell as they reached the edge of the subdivision. An old gas station offered temporary shelter—easily secured, with clear sightlines in all directions. She cleared it methodically, then barricaded the doors with shelving units and cinder blocks.

The girl watched her work, then mirrored her actions at the second entrance. Unprompted. Useful.

She built a small fire in a metal trash can, just enough for warmth without visible smoke. From her pack came the peanut butter. Half for now, half saved. The girl ate mechanically, eyes never leaving the windows.

"I'm Riley," the girl offered after finishing her portion.

She nodded acknowledgment but gave no name in return. Names created attachments. Attachments created vulnerabilities.

"You don't talk much," Riley observed. "That's okay. My mom talked all the time. Said everything twice. Dad said she'd lecture a fence post if it would listen."

The past tense. Already adjusting. Survivors adapted quickly or joined the dead.

She unrolled her sleeping mat and gestured for the girl to take it. Riley hesitated, then complied, curling into a tight ball beneath the jacket. Within minutes, exhaustion claimed her.

Sleep came in measured increments for the woman— twenty minutes at a time, alert for five, then repeat. The discipline had kept her alive for two winters already.

Morning arrived gray and threatening more snow. They moved out at first light, following the interstate but keeping to the treeline that ran parallel to it. Less exposed that way.

Riley kept pace without complaint. Once, when they spotted a trio of undead in the distance, the girl instinctively crouched and stilled. Quick learner.

By midday, they'd covered eight miles. Not enough. Weather was turning. The clouds hung low and heavy, pregnant with snow. They needed better shelter for the night.

A cluster of industrial buildings appeared on the horizon. Warehouses, loading docks. One had partially collapsed, but another stood intact, its metal walls offering protection from both elements and eyes.

The approach required crossing two hundred yards of open ground. She studied the terrain through compact binoculars. Nothing moved, but that meant little. The infected could remain motionless for hours when not stimulated.

She gestured for Riley to stay put, then crossed the first hundred yards in a low crouch, machete ready. Nothing stirred. She signaled the girl forward.

They were thirty yards from the warehouse door when the pack emerged—undead, not infected, shambling from behind a row of rusted shipping containers. A dozen at least, forming a loose semicircle.

Too many to fight in the open. Too spread out to outmaneuver. The warehouse remained their only option.

She grabbed Riley's sleeve and pointed. "Sprint," she whispered, breaking her silence for the first time. The tactical necessity outweighed habit. "Don't stop."

They ran. The undead followed with their maddening, implacable slowness. The warehouse door—a heavy sliding metal affair—stood partially open, just wide enough to slip through. They made it inside with fifty yards to spare.

The interior was cavernous, filled with abandoned shelving and forklifts. The loading bay doors were sealed, but smaller man-doors punctuated the walls at regular intervals. Too many access points to secure effectively.

"Up," she directed, pointing to a metal staircase that led to an office overlooking the warehouse floor. Defensible high ground with a single entry point.

The office had been ransacked long ago, but the fundamentals remained sound—solid walls, intact windows, and a heavy door. They barricaded it with a desk and filing cabinets as the first undead reached the warehouse floor below.

"We're safe here?" Riley asked.

Not safe. Never safe. Just safer. She nodded anyway.

Outside, the snow began to fall. A blessing in disguise. It would muffle sound and obscure their tracks when they moved on. The undead would grow sluggish in extreme cold, their decaying muscles stiffening with frost.

She used the remaining daylight to inspect and clean her weapons. The machete needed sharpening. The shotgun was empty, but she kept it—useful for intimidation, and ammunition might appear.

Riley watched her methodical weapons maintenance, then asked, "Can you teach me?"

She hesitated. Teaching meant investment. Investment meant attachment. Attachment meant vulnerability.

But the girl had already demonstrated aptitude. Had saved her life. Tactical pragmatism won out. She handed over the knife and demonstrated the proper sharpening technique on the machete. Riley mimicked her movements with careful precision.

The next three days followed a similar pattern. They moved north by day, found secure shelter by night. The snowfall intensified, then relented, leaving a foot of fresh powder that complicated travel but provided a clean slate to read threats upon.

Each day, she taught Riley another survival skill. How to move silently through different terrains. How to identify safe water sources. How to read the behavior patterns of the infected versus the undead. The girl absorbed everything, asking pointed questions that revealed a sharp mind.

On the fourth day, they encountered some human survivors—men with hunting rifles and hollow eyes. She spotted them from half a mile away, their orange hunting vests bright against the snow. Amateurs. Colors like that attracted both infected and predatory survivors.

She led Riley on a wide detour through denser woods. The men never knew they passed within a hundred yards of them.

"Why did we avoid them?" Riley asked afterward. "They had guns. They might have had food."

"People are unpredictable," she said, the most words she'd strung together yet. "The dead only want one thing. The living want everything."

The girl considered this, then nodded. "Like what happened to my mom and dad. They tried to help someone. The person was bleeding. They didn't know she was infected."

No more needed to be said. The story was common enough to be archetypal by now.

That night they sheltered in an abandoned church, sleeping in the bell tower where they could see approaches from all directions. As they ate the last of the peanut butter, Riley said, "I think we make a good team."

The statement hung in the air, dangerous in its implication. Teams meant permanence. Permanence meant vulnerability.

But somewhere in the frozen wasteland of her chest, something shifted. Not warmth, exactly. Recognition, perhaps. Of what she had been before. Of what the girl might become.

On the sixth day, they reached the outskirts of the mall. From their vantage point on a wooded hillside, they could see the camp—fifty or sixty people moving among makeshift structures. Guards patrolled the perimeter. Smoke rose from several cooking fires. Not just survival, but the beginnings of something like civilization.

Riley studied the scene intently. "We're going there? Together?"

She'd been preparing the answer for days. "You are."

The girl's face remained carefully neutral, but her eyes betrayed her. "Because I'll slow you down."

"Because you deserve more than just surviving."

They watched the camp in silence for an hour. It was as safe as anything could be in this world. Organized. Defensible. Community meant shared resources, shared knowledge. For a child, it offered possibilities beyond mere continued existence.

"Will you come back?" Riley asked finally. "To check on me?"

She met the girl's eyes. No false promises. No comforting lies. Just brutal honesty, the only gift she had to offer. "No."

Riley nodded slowly. "Because attachments are dangerous."

Perceptive kid.

They approached the camp's main entrance together. Guards raised weapons, then lowered them upon seeing the child. One stepped forward, rifle held non-threateningly across his chest.

"Looking for sanctuary?" he called.

She nudged Riley forward, keeping her own hands visible but ready near her weapons.

"Just for her," she answered. "She's uninfected. Quick learner. Useful."

The guard studied them both, understanding the situation immediately. It wasn't the first time this had happened. "We take care of our own here," he said. "Especially the kids."

Riley turned to her, eyes dry but chin trembling slightly. "Thank you for not leaving me there."

She allowed her hand to rest briefly on the girl's shoulder. The closest thing to tenderness she'd shown or felt in longer than she could remember. Then she stepped back, creating distance.

The guard extended his hand toward Riley. "Come on. We'll get you some hot food and a place to sleep."

Riley took a few steps toward the camp, then turned back. "You know, you don't have to be alone."

But she did. Solitude was survival. Attachment was vulnerability. The lesson had been written in blood too many times to ignore.

As Riley disappeared into the camp, she faded back into the treeline. The weight of her pack felt different somehow. Heavier, despite having given away supplies. A physical reminder of choices that couldn't be undone. She pushed the thought aside and focused on the horizon, checking the position of the sun. Four hours of daylight remained. Enough to put miles between herself and this moment of weakness.

She moved north again, into the endless white. One foot after another. No destination but distance. No companion but vigilance. No horizon but survival.

No Horizon: Scorched Earth

The wind shifted suddenly, bringing the acrid smell of smoke. She froze mid-stride, her hand instinctively tightening around the worn grip of her pump shotgun. Eyes narrowing, she scanned the western horizon where an ominous orange glow had begun to replace the setting sun.

Wildfire.

She pulled a bandana from her pocket, tying it around her face before moving to higher ground. From the abandoned gas station's roof, the situation became clear—a massive wall of flame devoured the forest five miles west, spreading rapidly across the drought-stricken landscape. The summer had been mercilessly dry, turning the region into perfect kindling.

Two problems immediately presented themselves: the main road north was already being consumed by the fire's leading edge, and thick plumes of black smoke were rolling eastward—directly toward her current position. The wind was picking up too, which meant the fire would accelerate.

She climbed down with meticulous speed, mentally cataloging her gear as she reached the ground. The pump shotgun with six shells. Machete strapped to her thigh. Handaxe and crowbar secured to her pack. Survival knife at her belt. Three liters of water. Enough food for four days if rationed. First aid supplies. Fire-starting tools that would be unnecessary in the coming hours.

A quick assessment of her surroundings confirmed what she already knew—this location would be overrun within hours. Moving east was the obvious choice, but escaping the fire wasn't her only concern. The advancing wall of flames would drive everything in its path forward—including the infected.

She'd need to move quickly, but carefully.

Two hours later, she crouched behind an overturned SUV, watching as a pack of seven infected stumbled along the road, driven forward by the approaching fire. Their erratic, twitching movements betrayed their nature—these weren't the reanimated dead but living hosts still in the grip of the first-stage infection. Fast, aggressive, and drawn to noise and movement.

The glow behind them had intensified, casting long, distorted shadows. Smoke thickened the air despite the bandana, making her eyes water. She remained motionless, controlling her breathing as the infected shambled past her position, their guttural moans barely audible over the distant roar of the fire.

Once they passed, she moved in the opposite direction of their trajectory, keeping low and using the smoke as additional cover. The fire was pushing everything eastward, but she needed to circle southeast to avoid the largest concentration of structures —and likely, the largest concentration of threats.

The outskirts of a small suburban development appeared through the haze. She paused at the edge of a cul-de-sac, assessing. Most houses showed signs of long abandonment— broken windows, weather-worn exteriors, yards returned to wilderness. One structure caught her attention: a two-story home

261

with intact solar panels on the roof and rain barrels at the corners. Someone had fortified this place, which meant it might contain useful supplies—or occupants.

She circled the property methodically, noting the boards over first-floor windows, the removed staircase rails that would make climbing to the second floor difficult, and the carefully arranged debris that would alert residents to intruders. Clever preparations, but no recent signs of habitation. No movement inside. No fresh tracks in the dust.

The rear entrance had been reinforced but showed damage from a previous attempted break-in. Using her crowbar, she carefully finished what others had started, ensuring the door opened silently. She entered with her shotgun raised, moving through the ground floor with cold precision.

The house was empty of life but contained valuable resources: a store of canned food, some medical supplies, ammunition that wouldn't fit her shotgun, and—most critically—a stored cache of bottled water and filtration equipment. The previous occupants had been prepared but had either moved on or met their end elsewhere.

A sudden crash from outside froze her in place. Through a narrow gap in the boarded windows, she spotted the source— three human figures moving through the neighboring yard, their voices carrying in urgent whispers.

"...fire's pushing them all this way. We need to grab what we can and move."

"Check that house with the solar setup. Has to be supplies in there."

She retreated to the kitchen, calculating. Raiders. Three confirmed, possibly more. They would be better armed than the infected but potentially more predictable. She could either engage or evade. Fighting meant noise, which would attract the infected being pushed ahead of the fire. Slipping away meant losing access to the valuable supplies.

Decision made, she moved quickly to the staircase landing, positioning herself above the entryway where she'd have both tactical advantage and clear sight lines to the door. From this elevated vantage point, she could strike first or retreat upstairs if needed. She waited, controlling her breathing as footsteps approached the house.

Ed Rodriguez

The first raider died without ever seeing her. As he stepped through the doorway, she brought the machete down from her position on the staircase landing, the blade slicing through his neck with practiced precision. She caught his body as it fell, lowering it silently to the floor.

"Frank? You find anything?" A voice called from outside.

She dragged the body into the shadows, retrieving the dead man's pistol and checking its load—five rounds remaining. Not her preferred weapon, but useful for the situation.

The second raider entered cautiously, weapon drawn. She waited until he turned toward the kitchen before dropping from the landing behind him. The handaxe made a dull thunk as it embedded in the base of his skull. She lowered this body too, moving with deliberate silence.

The third raider proved more cautious than his companions. He called out several times, then fired a warning shot through the doorway. She remained still, letting the silence stretch. Eventually, caution gave way to necessity—the approaching fire left little time for standoffs.

264

When he finally entered, she allowed him to spot the bodies of his companions before stepping into view with the pistol aimed at his chest.

"Wait—" he started, raising his hands.

The pistol made a sharp crack that would carry. She needed to move quickly now.

Gathering only what she could efficiently carry, she filled her pack with water bottles, medical supplies, and the most calorie-dense food items. She took the raiders' ammunition and a pair of binoculars but left their heavier weapons. From a bedroom closet, she retrieved a respirator mask with extra filters— essential equipment in a region where seasonal wildfires had been common even before the world ended. The home's solar panels and careful preparations suggested owners who had planned for all environmental threats, not just human ones.

As she exited through the back door, the first infected attracted by the gunshot rounded the corner of the house. Its milky eyes fixed on her as it charged with unnatural speed. Her machete severed its spinal cord with a single practiced stroke.

More would come. The fire was less than three miles away now, its roar audible even at this distance. She needed to keep moving southeast.

By nightfall, the situation had deteriorated significantly. The wind had intensified, driving the fire forward at an alarming rate. What should have been darkness was instead an eerie orange glow that backlit the smoke-filled sky. The air had grown nearly unbreathable despite her respirator, and burning embers carried on the wind ignited spot fires ahead of the main blaze.

She'd made good progress through the suburban sprawl, but now faced a critical obstacle—a ravine with only one crossing point, a bridge already crowded with infected fleeing the fire. At least thirty of them milled about, some freshly turned by the looks of their injuries, others in advanced stages of decomposition—the truly dead ones that only ceased with head trauma.

Backtracking wasn't an option with the fire advancing. Going around would take too long. The bridge was her only viable path.

She hunkered down behind an abandoned pickup truck, formulating a plan. Direct confrontation would be suicide, but the infected had predictable behaviors she could exploit. They were drawn to noise and movement but confused by multiple stimuli.

From her pack, she retrieved a small battery-operated radio salvaged months ago. It still had enough power for what she needed. Setting the volume to maximum, she placed it in the cab of another vehicle fifty yards from the bridge approach. Next, she gathered discarded bottles and created a rope of torn fabric from a nearby corpse.

With careful movements, she positioned herself on the far side of the bridge approach, then activated her makeshift diversion. The radio blared static, immediately drawing the infected toward the sound. When half had moved away from the bridge, she lit the fabric fuse on her Molotov cocktail and hurled it into the center of the remaining group.

The bottle shattered, spreading flames across three infected who screeched and flailed, creating further chaos. Predictably, the motion and sound drew the attention of those headed toward the radio. In the confusion, she sprinted for the bridge, machete in one hand, handaxe in the other.

Two infected blocked her path. The first lost its legs to a machete strike and fell screaming. The second reached for her with blackened fingers but met the handaxe instead, the blade crushing through its temple. She didn't break stride, vaulting over a stalled car and sprinting across the bridge as chaos erupted behind her.

Halfway across, a reanimated corpse lurched from behind a vehicle. No time for blade weapons—she drove her shoulder into its desiccated chest, sending it over the bridge railing into the ravine below. Three more steps and she encountered another, this one fresher and stronger. The handaxe connected with its forehead, but stuck in the bone. She abandoned the tool without hesitation, drawing her survival knife to dispatch a third infected before finally clearing the bridge.

Looking back, she saw the horde in disarray—some burning, some following the radio's noise, others now tracking her movement. Beyond them, the wildfire's front edge had reached the suburb's western border, setting structures ablaze. She turned southeast and continued moving, the orange glow reflecting off the sweat on her face.

Dawn brought no relief. The fire had advanced relentlessly through the night, and now a miles-wide inferno raged behind her. The wind still pushed east, carrying thick smoke and burning debris. Her respirator filter was clogging, making each breath a labor. Her eyes stung constantly despite the makeshift goggles she'd fashioned from a clear plastic container and elastic cord.

She'd reached what had once been a large commercial farm. The open fields offered less fuel for the wildfire but provided minimal cover from other threats. In the distance, farm buildings and silos stood like sentinels against the smoke-filled sky.

Her water supply had dwindled faster than anticipated due to the heat and exertion. Finding more had become her priority, even more urgent than outpacing the fire. The farm complex might offer both water and temporary shelter from the advancing blaze.

As she crossed the fallow fields, movement caught her eye—a small group of figures huddled near one of the outlying buildings. Through her scavenged binoculars, she identified four people—an older man, a woman about the same age, and two adolescents. They were loading supplies into a pickup truck with functional solar panels retrofitted to its hood and bed.

Survivors with resources and transportation.

She observed them for twenty minutes, noting their organized movements and defensive postures. They weren't raiders—their behavior showed the caution of people who avoided conflict rather than sought it. Still, approaching strangers always carried risk, especially when resources were involved.

The decision was made for her when the sound of an engine turned her attention to the road leading to the farm. A convoy of three vehicles approached rapidly—two motorcycles and a modified truck with reinforced bumpers and metal plates welded over the windows. Raiders, and well-equipped ones.

The family at the farm hadn't noticed yet, focused on their preparations. She had no obligation to them, no connection. Intervening meant risk and potential loss of supplies. The rational choice was to remain hidden and continue southeast.

Instead, she moved.

Keeping low in the field's tall grass, she circled to intercept the raiders before they reached the farm buildings. The two motorcycles had pulled ahead of the truck, their riders wearing makeshift armor of sports equipment and carrying machetes. One had a pistol holstered at his waist.

She positioned herself at the edge of a drainage ditch where the farm road narrowed between two equipment sheds. When the lead motorcycle passed, she remained still. As the second approached, she rose suddenly, shotgun leveled.

The thunderous blast threw the rider backward off his vehicle, which crashed into the ditch. The report echoed across the fields, eliminating any element of surprise. The lead rider skidded to a halt, turning his motorcycle around while drawing his pistol.

She was already moving, sliding into the drainage ditch as bullets kicked up dirt where she'd been standing. The truck engine roared as its driver accelerated toward her position. She pumped the shotgun's action and waited, timing her movements to the approaching sounds.

When the first motorcycle rider appeared at the edge of the ditch, weapon scanning for targets, she fired upward. The blast caught him under the chin, removing most of his head. His body toppled forward, the pistol falling into the ditch beside her.

The truck skidded to a halt thirty yards away. She heard doors opening, voices shouting orders. At least three more raiders. They would approach cautiously now, knowing they faced an armed opponent.

She retrieved the fallen pistol—a 9mm with a partially loaded magazine—and checked the shotgun. Four shells remaining. Not enough for a prolonged engagement.

The farm family had heard the commotion. Through gaps in the drainage culvert, she saw them taking defensive positions around their vehicle, weapons ready. Good. They weren't fleeing or surrendering.

A raider appeared at the far end of the ditch, firing repeatedly in her direction. The shots went wide, but forced her deeper into the culvert. Another approached from the opposite side, attempting to flank her position.

She fired the pistol twice toward the first raider, not aiming to hit but to make him take cover. Then she moved quickly toward the second, emerging from the ditch in a smooth motion that brought her face to face with a startled man wielding a baseball bat studded with nails.

The shotgun's blast tore through his chest before he could swing. Three shells left.

The remaining raiders began firing from multiple positions. She rolled behind a rusted tractor as bullets pinged off metal around her. The farm family had joined the fight now, laying down covering fire from their position. One raider fell to their shots.

She used the distraction to circle behind a storage shed, flanking the raiders' position. Through a gap in the wall, she spotted the truck driver—a large man with a tactical vest and assault rifle. The group's leader, judging by how he barked orders at the others.

Conserving ammunition, she retrieved the machete from her thigh holster and waited for him to move past her position. When he did, she struck from behind, driving the blade through the base of his skull with enough force to sever his brain stem. His body collapsed without a sound.

The last raider, seeing his leader fall, broke cover and ran for the truck. Multiple gunshots rang out from the farm family's position, dropping him before he reached the vehicle.

Silence fell across the farm, broken only by the distant roar of the approaching fire and the ringing in her ears from the gunfire.

"You saved our lives," the older man said as she approached their position, shotgun lowered but ready. "We've got room in the truck if you need a ride out. Fire's coming fast."

She studied their faces—weathered, cautious, but without the hardness typical of raiders or the desperation of recent survivors. They'd been making it work for some time. The solar-equipped truck showed ingenuity. The organized defense demonstrated experience.

Still, trusting strangers meant vulnerability.

The woman stepped forward, offering a canteen. "At least take some water. There's a river about fifteen miles southeast that should stop the fire's spread. That's where we're headed."

She accepted the water, drinking carefully while maintaining awareness of her surroundings. The fire had advanced visibly during the brief engagement, a wall of flame now consuming the western edge of the farmland. They had minutes, not hours.

"We've got a map," one of the adolescents said, holding up a weathered road atlas. "Shows the bridges that are still passable."

She hesitated, calculating. Joining them meant faster travel, shared resources, and strength in numbers. It also meant compromising her independence and trusting her survival to others' decisions.

Black smoke billowed overhead as the fire reached the field's edge. Ash rained down around them. The respirator's filter was nearly useless now. The flames would reach their position in minutes.

The older man climbed into the driver's seat without pushing further. "Offer stands. We're leaving now."

She made her decision, securing her shotgun across her back and retrieving the assault rifle from the fallen raider leader. The weapon was well-maintained with a half-full magazine—too valuable to leave behind.

As the family crowded into the truck's cab, she climbed into the bed, positioning herself where she could observe both the road ahead and behind. No words were exchanged as the engine rumbled to life and the truck accelerated away from the advancing inferno.

Through the swirling smoke and ash, she watched the farmland disappear into the flames. The fire continued its relentless advance, but for now, she had outpaced it. Tomorrow would bring new challenges—the river crossing, potential infected drawn by the fire, the inevitable moment when she would part ways with these temporary allies.

For now, she allowed herself one small liberty—removing the respirator for a moment to take a single, relatively clean breath as they outran the smoke. Her face, streaked with soot and dried blood, remained impassive. But as she secured the mask back in place, her fingers lingered briefly on a small metal object secured to her belt—a military-grade compass, its case worn from years of handling. She opened it with practiced precision, watching the needle stabilize before closing it with a soft click that seemed to carry personal weight beyond mere navigation.

Then her expression hardened once more, her eyes scanning the road ahead as the truck carried them toward the southeastern horizon, away from the fire that had consumed everything behind them, leaving no visible horizon—only smoke, ash, and flame.

Ed Rodriguez

No Horizon: The Last Trade

The dust came first, a thin veil of orange-brown that thickened the air and coated her lungs. She adjusted the respirator, tightening the seal around her face as she watched the trading post through her binoculars. Half a mile out, positioned on a rocky outcrop that offered both concealment and a tactical vantage point, she observed the bustling activity below with the detached focus of a predator.

Crosswinds Trading Post stood as an anomaly in the wasteland—a testament to preparation and leadership. Concrete barriers surrounded its perimeter, reinforced with corrugated metal and razor wire. Guard towers punctuated each corner, manned by sentries with scoped rifles. The main gate was a

279

masterpiece of scavenged engineering: a double-layered entry system with a decontamination chamber between barriers.

She lowered the binoculars, noting the change in the wind patterns. The dust storm was building faster than expected. Two days ago, she'd spotted the telltale signs of raider activity while making her way across the Midwest desert: fresh tire tracks veering off established routes, carrion birds circling execution sites, plumes of black smoke from burned homesteads. The raiders were moving with purpose, testing defenses, gathering intelligence. Crosswinds would be their next target.

Her visit had been planned weeks in advance—a rare indulgence in something resembling human connection. She hadn't expected to arrive with a warning of imminent attack.

Retrieving her pack, she checked her equipment methodically: pump-action shotgun, ammunition distributed evenly through various pockets for balanced weight, machete secured to her hip, handaxe and crowbar lashed to the exterior of the pack, survival knife in its ankle sheath. The weight was familiar, comforting in its utility.

She began her approach as the wind intensified, using the brewing storm as additional cover. Visibility would soon drop to near zero—a tactical advantage for someone who knew the terrain and a death sentence for those who didn't.

Three hundred yards from the main gate, she froze. Movement to the southeast, barely visible through the thickening haze. She dropped prone, digging her elbows into the sand as she raised the binoculars again.

A scout party—three vehicles moving in a staggered formation, using the terrain for concealment. The lead vehicle stopped periodically, allowing a figure to exit and survey the land ahead with what appeared to be a spotting scope. They were mapping approach vectors, identifying blind spots in Crosswinds' defenses.

She marked their position mentally, calculating time and distance. She'd tracked similar scouts yesterday to their main force in the dry riverbed east. Based on the tracks she'd seen, she estimated thirty to forty raiders—a substantial force with vehicle-mounted weapons and enough manpower to overwhelm Crosswinds if the attack came as a surprise.

The gate loomed ahead as she completed her approach. A voice called down from the guard tower.

"Identify yourself!"

She raised a hand slowly, then removed her respirator, exposing her face to the stinging sand. Recognition came quickly.

"Open the gate! It's Crosswinds' ghost."

The nickname had always amused her—a reference to her habit of appearing without warning and leaving just as suddenly. The inner workings of the gate groaned as the mechanisms engaged, creating a gap just wide enough for one person to slip through.

Inside the decontamination chamber, she submitted to the security protocol without complaint—turning out her pockets, allowing the guard to check her pack, demonstrating that she wasn't infected by removing her jacket to reveal unbitten arms. Standard procedure, performed with the efficiency of long practice.

The inner gate opened, revealing Crosswinds proper—a network of repurposed shipping containers and concrete structures arranged in concentric rings around a central courtyard. Solar panels covered many of the rooftops, and water collection systems funneled into central cisterns. Gardens grew in protected enclosures, their plastic coverings cloudy with age but still functional.

"Well, look what the storm blew in."

She turned toward the familiar voice. Lewis Taylor stood at the entrance to the command center, arms crossed over his chest, the ghost of a smile playing at the corners of his mouth. He'd aged since she'd seen him last—more grey in his beard, deeper lines around his eyes—but he moved with the same easy confidence that had first drawn her attention years ago.

Her heartbeat quickened traitorously. She nodded once in acknowledgment, then gestured toward the command center with a tilt of her head. The smile faded from Lewis's face as he read her expression.

"Trouble?" he asked quietly.

"Raiders," she said simply. Unlike with everyone else, words came easier with Lewis. She stepped inside as he moved aside.

Inside, maps covered the walls—detailed surveys of the surrounding fifty miles, marked with known hazards, infected zones, and resource caches. She moved directly to the southeastern quadrant, pointing to the area where she'd spotted the scout party.

Lewis leaned in, studying the map. "How many?"

"Three scout vehicles I spotted," she said, her voice low and measured. "Main force hiding in the dry riverbed five miles east. About forty, based on the tracks."

"Forty? You're certain?"

"Yes." She began to sketch in the dust on the table—a rough diagram of vehicles positioned for an attack. "Small convoy here for diversion. Armored battering ram targeting the main gate, rigged with explosives." The tactical plan became clear through her swift, economical movements and terse explanation.

Lewis's face hardened as he grasped the strategy. "When?"

She pointed upward, toward the howling wind, then swept her hand horizontally—during the storm. Maximum cover, minimum visibility for defenders.

"We've got maybe two hours before it hits full force," Lewis said, already moving toward the radio. "Johnson, sound condition yellow. All civilians to shelters, defense teams to stations. Full perimeter check, double ammunition at all posts."

She watched him work, issuing orders with calm efficiency. This was why Crosswinds survived while other communities fell—Lewis's ability to inspire confidence while making hard decisions.

He turned back to her. "I need to know everything you saw. Every detail."

"They're well-equipped," she said, her words reserved only for him. "Military-grade weapons. Coordinated movements." For the next twenty minutes, she relayed her observations, mixing terse sentences with gestures and drawings. The scout party's movement patterns. The type of vehicles in use. The weapons she'd observed. The likely staging area for the main force.

Lewis absorbed it all, adjusting the defense plan accordingly. When she indicated a blind spot in the southeastern perimeter—a dip in the terrain that could conceal an approach—he immediately assigned additional guards to the area.

"You didn't have to warn us," he said finally, studying her with an intensity that made her want to look away. "Could have bypassed us entirely, avoided the risk."

"I was coming here anyway," she said quietly, uncomfortable with the implicit question. Her reasons for coming to Crosswinds hadn't changed, but they weren't relevant to the immediate threat. She pointed to the map again, then to herself. "I'll help defend the south wall."

Lewis nodded slowly. "We could use you on the south wall. Best sight lines, most likely direction for the main thrust."

"I still need supplies," she said, gesturing toward the trading post's stores. The transaction would proceed as planned, regardless of the impending attack.

"Take what you need," Lewis said. "Put it on my account."

The offer surprised her. She shook her head firmly, reaching into her pocket to produce a small leather pouch. "No. Fair trade." She emptied the contents onto the table: antibiotics, salvaged from a pharmacy two states over. Worth their weight in gold.

Lewis's eyebrows rose. "Where did you—" He stopped himself, knowing better than to ask. "Fine. Equal trade. But if we survive this, we're sharing a drink afterward."

"Just like old times," she replied, the wisp of a smile playing at her lips.

Something stirred in her chest—a warmth she ruthlessly suppressed. She gathered the antibiotics, returning all but two vials to her pouch, then laid those on the table as payment. Lewis accepted with a nod, no further discussion needed.

She exited the command center, heading directly for the marketplace. The storm's approach had created a flurry of activity as shopkeepers secured their goods and residents hurried toward the central shelters. She moved against the flow, focused on acquiring what she needed before taking her position on the wall.

The apothecary first—antiseptic, bandages, suture kits. Then the provisioner for dried meat, purification tablets, and storm-proof matches. She bartered efficiently, trading small luxuries she'd scavenged on her journey—a silver bracelet, a functioning watch, packets of spices—for necessities. Each transaction was quick, impersonal, yet she noted how the vendors nodded respectfully, offering their best goods without the usual haggling. Word of the coming attack had spread.

As she filled her pack, the wind grew stronger. Sand particles stung any exposed skin, forcing residents to don goggles and wrap scarves around their faces. The world narrowed to a sepia-toned haze, buildings reduced to looming shadows.

Perfect conditions for an attack.

She made her way to the south wall, climbing the metal stairs to the guard platform. Three defenders were already in position, checking weapons and adjusting their protective gear. They nodded to her but asked no questions. Her reputation preceded her.

From her vantage point, she could see approximately fifty yards into the storm before visibility dropped to zero. She unslung her shotgun, checking the action, then positioned herself at the corner of the platform, where the southwest and south walls met. If the raiders followed the plan she'd outlined, the initial diversion would come from directly south, while the armored battering ram would approach from the southwest, using the confusion to break through the main gate.

The first hour passed in tense silence. The storm reached its peak, howling around the outpost's walls, rattling the metal sheets and drowning out all but the loudest communications. She remained motionless, conserving energy, eyes scanning methodically through the swirling dust.

Then—a flicker of movement. She raised her hand, alerting the other defenders. Three shadows emerged from the storm, moving in a triangular formation. The diversionary force, right on schedule.

She held her fire, tracking their movement. Let them come closer, reveal their full strength before engaging. The lead vehicle—a pickup truck with a mounted gun—crept forward, advancing to within thirty yards of the wall.

The attack came with sudden ferocity. Machine gun fire raked the top of the wall as raiders leapt from the vehicles, using the cover of the storm to rush forward with grappling hooks and makeshift ladders.

She responded with practiced precision, the shotgun's report a muffled boom in the howling wind. A raider dropped, his grappling hook falling uselessly to the ground. She ejected the spent shell, chambered another round, and fired again. Another raider down.

The outpost's defenders returned fire, lead projectiles cutting through the dust-filled air. A raider vehicle exploded as a molotov cocktail arced from the wall, the flames momentarily illuminating the battlefield before being swallowed by the storm.

But this was just the diversion. She scanned to the southwest, ignoring the chaos directly in front of her. There—a massive shadow pulling into position. The armored truck, its engine barely audible over the storm, positioning itself for a run at the main gate.

She tapped the shoulder of the nearest defender, pointing urgently toward the new threat. The defender's eyes widened as he spotted the vehicle, then he turned and sprinted toward the command center to raise the alarm.

She didn't wait. Slinging the shotgun across her back, she moved quickly along the wall toward a maintenance ladder that would give her access to the ground near the southwest corner. Time was critical—the truck would begin its run any second, and once it gained momentum, nothing short of heavy weaponry would stop it.

Descending the ladder, she dropped the final six feet to the ground, landing in a crouch. The truck's engine roared as it began to accelerate. She had seconds at most.

Her hand went to her belt, retrieving the handaxe. Not ideal, but she needed something with enough heft to cause damage. She sprinted through the swirling dust, positioning herself just inside the outpost's perimeter, close to where the truck would hit the gate.

The massive vehicle materialized from the storm like a charging bull, its reinforced front end bristling with welded metal spikes. The gate would never hold against such force.

She waited until the last possible moment, then darted forward, timing her movement to coincide with the truck's impact. As metal crashed against metal, she leapt onto the side of the vehicle, finding purchase on the external frame welded to its body.

The truck smashed through the outer gate, momentum carrying it forward into the decontamination chamber. She climbed quickly, making her way toward the cab as the driver gunned the engine, preparing to break through the inner gate.

Reaching the roof, she quickly assessed the vehicle's weaknesses. The cabin was armored, but there was a gap where the roof met the windshield—a vulnerability. She retrieved her crowbar, wedging it into the seam and applying leverage with all her strength.

Metal screamed as it bent, creating a gap just large enough. Without hesitation, she dropped a small object through the opening—one of the grenades she'd bartered for at the marketplace. Then she rolled off the truck, hitting the ground hard and scrambling away as quickly as possible.

The explosion ripped through the cabin, sending shrapnel and body parts flying in all directions. The truck swerved, its dead driver slumped over the wheel, and crashed into the wall of the decontamination chamber.

But the damage had been done. The outer gate hung from a single hinge, and the inner gate was buckled from the impact. Worse, she now saw the second part of the raiders' plan: explosives lined the truck's undercarriage, enough to blow a hole through both remaining barriers.

She reached the truck again, sliding underneath to access the explosive array. Simple remote detonators, designed to be triggered from a distance once the vehicle was in position. She traced the wires quickly, identifying the receiver. No time to disarm properly—she yanked the device free, breaking the connection.

The sound of engines growing louder told her the gambit had partially succeeded. The follow-up force was approaching, ready to pour through the breach once the explosives cleared the way. Without the detonation, they'd be forced to navigate the damaged but still partially intact gates—a bottleneck that would give the defenders a chance.

She rolled clear of the truck just as gunfire erupted. Raiders on motorcycles and in lightweight dune buggies swarmed into the decontamination chamber, weapons blazing. She drew her machete, taking cover behind the wrecked truck as bullets pinged off its armored shell.

A raider rounded the truck's bumper, shotgun raised. She struck first, the machete slicing through his forearm with practiced precision. As he screamed, dropping his weapon, she swept his legs from under him and finished the job with a strike to the throat.

She claimed his shotgun, checking its action—a semi-automatic, five shells remaining. A significant upgrade from her pump-action in this close-quarters situation.

The battle devolved into a chaotic melee as raiders attempted to force their way through the damaged inner gate while Crosswinds' defenders concentrated their fire on the bottleneck. She moved through the shadows of the decontamination chamber, using the raiders' vehicles as cover, picking off targets of opportunity with brutal efficiency.

Three raiders attempted to place additional explosives on the inner gate. She took down two with quick shotgun blasts, then engaged the third in hand-to-hand as her weapon ran dry. The raider lunged with a serrated combat knife. She deflected with her machete, then countered with a savage strike from her handaxe, burying it in his skull.

More raiders poured in from outside, overwhelming the defenders through sheer numbers. The inner gate began to buckle as they rammed it repeatedly with one of their vehicles.

She needed to change the equation. Surveying the decontamination chamber, she spotted the answer—the fuel tanks of the raiders' vehicles. Moving quickly, she retrieved one of her remaining molotov cocktails, lighting the rag wick with a stormproof match.

The bottle arced through the air, shattering against a dune buggy's exposed engine. Flames erupted instantly, spreading to nearby vehicles as their fuel tanks ruptured in the heat. Raiders scattered, caught between the inferno and the defenders' concentrated fire.

The tide turned suddenly. Organized defense overcame the chaotic attack as raiders broke ranks, attempting to flee back through the outer gate. Those who made it encountered a new threat—Lewis Taylor had led a flanking party around the outpost's exterior, using the storm as cover to circle behind the raiders' position.

Caught in a crossfire, the raiders' assault collapsed entirely. Within minutes, the survivors were retreating into the storm, leaving their dead and wounded behind.

She stood in the center of the decontamination chamber, surrounded by carnage, and for a moment allowed herself to feel the satisfaction of survival. The storm still raged outside, but within the outpost's walls, a fragile security had been preserved.

Lewis entered through the ruined outer gate, rifle in hand, face streaked with blood and dust. His eyes found hers immediately, and something passed between them— acknowledgment, respect, perhaps something more.

"We've pushed them back," he said, approaching her. "Scouts report they're in full retreat, at least six vehicles burning on the access road."

She nodded, cleaning her machete methodically before returning it to its sheath.

"That trick with the grenades," Lewis continued, "saved us all. The explosives under that truck would have taken out half the marketplace."

She shrugged, downplaying her role. Anyone would have done the same, given the opportunity.

"We're organizing repair teams now," he said. "Should have the gates functional again before the storm passes." He paused, studying her face. "You still planning to move on once it clears?"

The question hung between them, weighted with unspoken history. Three years ago, she'd stayed for nearly a month—the longest she'd remained anywhere since the world ended. They'd grown close, closer than she'd allowed herself to be with anyone since. Then the nightmares had returned, driving her back to the road, to the solitary existence that kept her demons at bay.

"I can't stay, Lewis," she said softly. "You know why."

Disappointment flickered across Lewis's features, quickly masked by understanding. "At least stay until repairs are complete. We owe you that much."

"My pack," she said, nodding toward the outpost's walls where she'd left it. "I need those supplies for the road."

"Already taken care of," Lewis said. "Everything you traded for, plus some extras. Consider it hazard pay."

The corner of her mouth twitched—almost a smile. She nodded her acceptance.

"And that drink I mentioned?" Lewis added, reaching into his jacket to produce a dusty bottle. "Figured now's as good a time as any."

The label was faded but legible: twenty-year-old scotch, a relic of the world before. He offered it to her first, an unexpected courtesy that stirred something long dormant inside her.

She accepted the bottle, taking a measured sip before passing it back. "Good stuff," she murmured. The liquor burned pleasantly, warming her from within. For just a moment, she allowed herself to remember what it had been like, during that month three years ago. The closest thing to peace she'd found in this broken world.

They shared the bottle as the cleanup began around them, their conversation sparse but meaningful. Raiders' bodies were dragged away for disposal, vehicles salvaged for parts, wounded treated in the medical bay. The easy rhythm of their interaction required few words, a comfort she had found with no one else.

"I missed this," she admitted quietly. "Missed you."

As twilight approached, the storm began to wane. The wind died down gradually, the air clearing of dust. She knew it was time to move on, before attachment took deeper root.

She gathered her pack, now restocked and ready for the journey ahead. Lewis walked her to the damaged gate, where temporary barriers had been erected until proper repairs could begin.

"You know you always have a place here," he said quietly, voice rough with emotion he rarely displayed.

She nodded, allowing herself to meet his gaze directly. "Be careful, Lewis," she said softly. In that moment of connection, something passed between them—an acknowledgment of what might have been in a different world, under different circumstances.

Lewis stepped forward suddenly, reaching for her hand. She allowed the contact, brief though it was. He pressed something into her palm—a small object wrapped in cloth.

"Just in case," he said.

She unwrapped it carefully: a compass, military grade, with a custom modification—a small compartment built into the base that contained a handwritten map of safe routes through the territories to the north.

The gift was practical yet deeply personal—acknowledging her need to keep moving while providing a way back, should she choose to take it. Her throat tightened unexpectedly.

"Thank you," she whispered, tucking the compass into her pocket. She reached out, briefly touching his face—a gesture of gratitude and farewell combined. "I'll be back. Eventually."

Without looking back, she stepped through the gate and into the clearing night.

The wind had sculpted the landscape during the storm, creating new dunes and exposing long-buried debris. She oriented herself using the emerging stars, setting a course northeast. Five miles out, she would make camp in the remains of an abandoned gas station she'd scouted on her approach.

Tomorrow would bring new challenges, new threats to overcome. She would face them as she always did—alone, relying on skills honed through years of brutal experience.

But as she walked away from Crosswinds Trading Post, the weight of the compass in her pocket reminded her that solitude was, at least for now, a choice rather than a necessity. The thought sustained her as she disappeared into the darkness, leaving no footprints in the newly settled dust.

The radio transmission came three days later, crackling through the static on the emergency frequency she monitored each evening.

"...attacked at dawn... overwhelming force... requesting any assistance..."

She recognized Lewis's voice immediately, strained with pain and urgency.

"...Lewis Taylor of Crosswinds... critically wounded... raiders have breached the inner perimeter..."

Her hand froze on the dial. Something cold settled in her stomach as the transmission continued.

"...anyone who can hear this... Crosswinds has fallen... do not approach... repeat... do not..."

The transmission cut off abruptly, leaving only static.

She sat motionless beside her small campfire, the familiar weight of her weapons suddenly insufficient against the hollowness expanding inside her chest. The compass lay in her open palm, its housing oriented so that southwest—toward Crosswinds—was clearly marked on the dial.

"I should have been there," she whispered to the empty night. "I could have saved you."

The regret hit her with physical force—if she hadn't left, if she'd stayed just one more day, Lewis might still be alive. She could have spotted the raiders' return, could have helped prepare defenses, could have protected him as she'd protected the outpost before.

Methodically, she began to pack her equipment, dousing the fire and erasing all evidence of her presence. The night was young, and if she traveled without rest, she could reach the outpost by dawn.

What she would find there, she already knew. The aftermath of slaughter. Bodies to bury. Perhaps survivors to aid, though the transmission left little hope of that.

Lewis would be among the dead. The thought came with a clarity that surprised her—not denial or bargaining, but simple, cold certainty. Another person gone. Another connection severed.

"You deserved better," she said, her voice breaking. "I should have been there."

Yet she would go back. Not to fight a battle already lost. Not even to seek vengeance, though that would come later, in its time. She would return because some debts could only be repaid in person, even when the creditor no longer lived to collect.

As she shouldered her pack and set out into the darkness, she allowed herself a moment of unprecedented weakness—a single tear, quickly absorbed by the dusty bandana covering her face. Then she moved forward, each step carrying her toward Crosswinds and whatever remained of the man who had dared to believe she might someday stay.

The horizon stretched before her, empty of promise but demanding survival nonetheless. She would endure. She always did.

It was what came after endurance that remained, as ever, uncertain.

No Horizon: Blood and Stone

The fever hit with the suddenness of a summer storm. One moment she was setting snares in the misty dawn light, the next her vision blurred and her skin felt as if it were peeling away from her muscles. She staggered, barely catching herself against the rough bark of a pine tree. The rabbit meat from the night before. It must have been tainted.

Her pack felt impossibly heavy as she tried to make her way back to the abandoned ranger station she'd secured three days prior. The shotgun slung across her back might as well have been an anchor, dragging her down with each lurching step. She'd gone no more than half a mile when her legs finally betrayed her, buckling beneath her weight.

303

As consciousness slipped away, she had just enough presence of mind to drag herself beneath the hollow of a fallen oak. Her last coherent thought was of the loaded shotgun clutched against her chest, her finger resting just outside the trigger guard.

Consciousness returned in fragments, like pieces of a broken mirror. Light filtering through fabric. The smell of wood smoke. Pain, dull and throbbing, radiating from every joint. Her mouth tasted of copper and ash. Something cool and damp pressed against her forehead.

She tried to move and found her limbs unnaturally heavy.

"Easy now. The fever's broken, but you're still weak."

The voice belonged to a man, gruff and weathered. She forced her eyes open, wincing against the light. A lean face with a salt-and-pepper beard came into focus. Late fifties, perhaps. Deep creases around pale blue eyes that assessed her with clinical detachment.

"Three days you've been out. Thought we'd lost you a couple times."

We. The word registered as a threat before her mind could fully process it. Her hand instinctively moved to her hip where her knife should have been. Nothing.

"Looking for your gear?" The man nodded toward the far side of what she now recognized as a small cabin. "Had to strip you down when the fever peaked. You were burning up, soaked through."

She took quick inventory. She lay on a cot covered by a thin blanket. Beneath it, she wore nothing. Her weapons, her pack, her clothes—all gone.

A second figure moved into view. A boy, perhaps sixteen, lanky with close-cropped hair and wary eyes. He carried a steaming mug that he set down beside the cot before retreating to a stool in the corner.

"Willow bark tea," the older man explained. "Best thing for fever. I'm Marcus. That's Eli. Found you half-dead in the woods while checking our trapline."

She remained silent, mentally cataloging escape routes, obstacles, potential weapons.

"Not much for talking? That's fine." Marcus settled onto a wooden chair. "World these days, caution keeps you alive. Drink your tea. Get your strength back."

She reached for the mug, keeping the blanket clutched to her chest with her other hand. The tea was bitter but warm. As she drank, she surveyed the cabin. Single room. Two windows, both shuttered. Door to her right. A wood stove. Simple furnishings. Her eyes stopped at a familiar shape propped in the corner—her shotgun.

"Your weapons are unloaded," Marcus said, following her gaze. "Standard precaution. You understand."

She nodded once, expression neutral despite the rising unease in her gut.

"Rest now," Marcus stood. "We'll talk more when you're stronger."

By the second day, she could sit up without the room spinning. Marcus brought her clothes—not her own, but a flannel shirt and cargo pants that hung loose on her frame.

"Your clothes were filthy," he explained. "Burned them. Disease prevention."

When she asked about her pack with a gesture, Marcus shook his head.

"Had to bury most of it. Blood and vomit soaked through everything. Couldn't risk contamination."

Her expression remained carefully blank, but inwardly, her suspicion hardened into certainty. The carefully arranged excuses. The delayed return of her weapons. The constant presence of either Marcus or Eli in the cabin.

She was not a guest. She was a prisoner.

That night, she feigned sleep while listening to Marcus and Eli talk in low voices by the stove.

"...could use someone like her," Marcus was saying. "Saw those calluses on her hands. The scars. She's a survivor."

"What if she doesn't want to stay?" Eli's voice, uncertain.

"Everyone needs people, son. Even her. She just doesn't know it yet."

She heard the clink of metal—her survival knife being handled.

"Custom job," Marcus murmured appreciatively. "Good balance. Someone taught her well."

"When do we give her stuff back?"

A pause. "We don't. Not yet. People get attached to their gear. Makes them think they don't need anything else."

She closed her eyes as footsteps approached. Marcus stood over her for a long moment before returning to his chair.

For three more days, she played along. She ate their food. Nodded at their explanations. Feigned weakness while secretly testing her returning strength. All the while, she observed.

Marcus was skilled—a hunter by trade before the world ended, he claimed. Competent with the lever-action rifle he carried, which she noted had been modified with a modern suppressor—explaining how he could hunt without drawing infected. Methodical in checking snares and preparing game. But his caution wavered when he thought she was warming to them. He began to stand closer. To touch her shoulder or arm when speaking. His eyes lingered too long.

Eli was different. Skittish and deferential to Marcus, who he called "sir" rather than father or uncle. The boy watched her with a mixture of fascination and fear. When Marcus was outside,

Eli would sometimes whisper fragments of information—where they kept ammunition, which floorboard creaked, how far to the nearest stream.

On the fourth night, Marcus brought back a doe. As they ate venison steaks by lantern light, he placed his hand on her knee.

"We work well together," he said, voice dropping low. "Three of us could make a proper go of it. Better than being alone out there."

She nodded, eyes downcast, the picture of submission. When his hand moved higher, she didn't resist.

"Been a long time since I had a woman around," he murmured. "Even longer since Eli here has seen one. Think we could make you comfortable."

The implication hung in the air like smoke. Her eyes flicked to the knife on Marcus' belt—her knife. Then to her shotgun, still propped in the corner. She forced a small smile and nodded.

Marcus grinned, squeezing her thigh. "See? Told you she'd come around, Eli."

The boy stared at his plate, shoulders hunched.

"Why don't you check the perimeter, son?" Marcus suggested, not taking his eyes off her. "Make sure we're secure for the night."

After a moment's hesitation, Eli shuffled outside. The instant the door closed, Marcus moved closer.

"Been patient," he growled. "Nursed you back. Fed you. Protected you. Time to show some gratitude."

She nodded again, then pointed to her throat and made a drinking motion.

"Thirsty?" Marcus chuckled. "Sure thing, darlin'."

He turned to reach for the water jug. In one fluid motion, she grabbed the cast iron skillet from beside the stove and brought it down on the back of his head with every ounce of her recovered strength.

Marcus crumpled forward, stunned but not unconscious. She struck again, harder. This time he stayed down. Blood pooled beneath his head as she quickly searched his pockets, retrieving her survival knife.

She moved with battle-tested movements. Her shotgun next. A box of shells from the shelf. Her boots by the door. She was lacing them when the door opened and Eli stood frozen in the threshold, eyes wide at the scene before him.

"He—he was going to keep you," the boy stammered. "Said you'd be our new family."

She said nothing, continuing to prepare. Food in a sack. Water bottle. Matches.

"He found others before," Eli continued, voice quavering. "They didn't last."

She paused, meeting the boy's eyes for the first time. Something passed between them—an understanding. Then she returned to gathering supplies.

"I can't let you take our stuff," Eli said, his voice hardening as he raised Marcus's rifle. "He'll kill me if I do."

She assessed the boy. The trembling hands. The uncertain stance. The desperate eyes of someone who'd been under another's control for too long.

Before Eli could steady his aim, she was across the room. One hand clamped around the rifle barrel, forcing it upward as her other hand brought the knife to his throat. They stood locked in a terrible tableau, her eyes boring into his.

His lower lip trembled. "Please," he whispered. "I don't know how to survive alone."

For an instant, something like compassion flickered across her face. Then Marcus groaned from the floor, and the moment shattered.

She disarmed Eli with a sharp twist, shoving him aside. Grabbing her partially filled sack, she backed toward the door. The boy made no move to follow as she disappeared into the night.

The forest absorbed her like water into soil. Moving with a speed born of desperation, she navigated the moonlit terrain, instinctively seeking higher ground. Two miles east, then north through a rocky ravine. The shotgun's familiar weight against her back centered her, its presence a talisman against the darkness.

She'd been running for nearly an hour when she heard it— a distant roar of primal rage echoing through the forest.

Marcus was awake. And he was hunting.

A cold certainty settled in her chest. This was not a man who would give up. Not a man who would be outsmarted easily.

With each passing minute, her assessment of his skills had grown. The way he moved through the forest. The precision of his traps. The calculating intelligence behind those pale eyes.

She'd escaped predators before—infected, undead, human. None had unnerved her like Marcus.

Dawn crept across the sky as she reached a swift-flowing stream. She waded upstream for half a mile, careful to leave no trace of her passage on either bank. Finding a fallen tree that stretched across the water, she used it as a bridge, then doubled back along a rocky ridge.

The deception would buy her time, but not much. She needed more.

She'd just begun setting a false trail leading west when a rifle shot struck with deadly quiet. The bullet splintered bark inches from her head.

Instinct drove her into a roll, seeking cover behind a moss-covered boulder. Another shot punched into the earth where she'd been a second before.

"Impressive," Marcus's voice carried across the distance. "Most people, their first instinct is to run. Not you. You move like someone who's been hunted before."

She controlled her breathing, calculating angles. The voice came from the northeast, perhaps two hundred yards away. Higher ground. He'd have sight lines to any movement.

"That knock to the head? Just made me angry." His voice shifted position slightly. He was moving, using speech to mask his approach. "Could've killed me. Should've killed me. That's going to cost you."

She gauged distances, mapped escape routes. The boulder provided cover, but it was also a trap. She needed to move before he closed the distance.

"I know these woods. Every tree, every stream, every cave." Another shift in position. "You're in my territory now."

She spotted a dense thicket of brambles thirty yards to her left. Too exposed to reach directly. She'd need a distraction.

Unslinging the shotgun, she removed a shell, carefully extracted the shot, and scattered the small lead pellets into her palm. With a flick of her wrist, she tossed them into the underbrush to her right.

The metallic patter drew an immediate response—two rapid rifle shots targeted where the sound originated. She was already moving, staying low, using the moment of distraction to reach the briar patch.

Thorns tore at her clothes as she wormed deeper into the thicket. Through gaps in the vegetation, she caught glimpses of movement. Marcus, moving with predatory grace despite his limp, rifle held ready. Eli trailed behind him like a shadow, carrying a pack and what looked like a machete.

"Hide all you want," Marcus called out. "Just makes the hunt more interesting. Been a while since I had prey that's actually challenging."

She remained motionless as he drew closer to her position. Twenty yards. Fifteen. Ten. The shotgun would be effective at this range, but the noise would draw every infected for miles. Better to wait, to let him pass.

Marcus stopped eight yards from her hiding place. His head turned slowly, nostrils flaring as if trying to scent her. For a terrible moment, she thought he'd spotted her. Then he signaled to Eli.

"Circle around that ridge," he ordered quietly. "Flush her toward the drop-off. I'll be waiting."

315

They were boxing her in. She watched as Eli moved away, leaving Marcus alone. An opportunity, but one laden with risk. She'd seen enough to know Marcus was no ordinary hunter. His movements were too calculated, his senses too attuned to the forest.

She waited until Eli disappeared from view, then began to slowly, silently extricate herself from the opposite side of the thicket. Each movement was measured, deliberate, minimizing the rustle of branches.

She'd nearly cleared the brambles when her foot dislodged a small stone. The sound was barely audible, but in the morning stillness, it might as well have been a gunshot.

Marcus spun, rifle raised, firing in one fluid motion.

The bullet tore through her jacket sleeve, grazing her upper arm. She ducked and rolled as a second shot kicked up dirt where she'd been. No time for stealth now. She sprinted for a cluster of boulders, zigzagging to make herself a harder target.

Two more shots followed, each closer than the last. Marcus was leading her, anticipating her movements. The fourth bullet clipped her calf, sending a hot lance of pain up her leg.

She stumbled but didn't fall, diving behind the rocks as a fifth shot ricocheted off stone inches from her head. Blood seeped through her pant leg—not arterial, but enough to leave a trail. Pressing her palm against the wound, she tried to stem the bleeding.

"First blood," Marcus called out, satisfaction evident in his voice. "That's how it always starts."

She heard him moving, circling to flank her position. The pain in her leg sharpened her focus. She'd been in worse situations. Had survived worse odds. This was just another day in a world designed to kill her.

Checking the shotgun, she calculated her options. The terrain sloped sharply to her right—a steep hillside leading down to what sounded like a larger stream. Behind her, more forest, but too exposed. To her left, the ridgeline Marcus had mentioned, where Eli would be waiting.

The hillside, then. Risky, but unpredictable.

She waited for the sound of Marcus moving between positions, then launched herself down the slope. The descent was controlled chaos—half running, half sliding down the loose soil and rocks. Her injured leg threatened to buckle with each impact, but momentum carried her forward.

Halfway down, a suppressed shot from Marcus's rifle sent a bullet past her. A miss, but close enough that she felt the bullet's passage displace the air near her face. She didn't look back, focusing instead on navigating the treacherous slope.

The ground suddenly disappeared beneath her feet. A hidden drop-off, concealed by undergrowth. She fell hard, tumbling the last ten feet to land awkwardly on a gravel riverbank.

Pain exploded through her right shoulder as it absorbed the impact. Dislocated, possibly. She bit back a cry, rolling to her knees. The shotgun had fallen several feet away. As she reached for it, a bullet kicked up gravel beside her hand.

"Impressive," Marcus called from the top of the ridge. "But predictable. I was hoping you'd take the slope."

She snatched up the shotgun with her good arm, diving behind a fallen tree as another shot splintered wood inches above her head. The pain in her shoulder made it difficult to aim, but she managed to chamber a round.

"You're wondering if you should use that shotgun," Marcus continued, his voice carrying easily across the distance as he began making his way down. "But we both know what happens if you do. Every infected within miles will come running. You'd be trading me for a hundred hungry mouths."

He was right. The noise would be a death sentence in infected territory. But the alternative—being hunted down by this predator—seemed equally final.

A new sound caught her attention—the distinctive gurgle and moan of an infected, somewhere downstream. Not close, but not far enough. Marcus had chosen hunting grounds near a hotzone deliberately.

"Hear that?" he called out. "Got a whole nest of them about half a mile downriver. Eli and I cleared a safe corridor coming in, but they're thick everywhere else. You fire that shotgun, you're dead either way."

She weighed her options. The stream offered a path, but also exposure. The forest on either side provided cover, but slower progress. And every minute increased the chance of her blood trail leading Marcus—or worse, infected—straight to her.

Decision made, she shrugged off her jacket, tying it tightly around her wounded leg to control the bleeding. The dislocated shoulder would have to wait. Using the fallen tree as cover, she edged toward the water, staying low.

When Marcus fired again—a ranging shot aimed at where he thought she might be—she took her chance. Abandoning the shotgun would be suicide, so she slung it awkwardly across her back and slipped into the stream. The shock of cold water nearly took her breath away, but it would help mask her scent and blood trail.

Moving downstream with the current, she stayed close to the bank where overhanging branches provided some cover. Each movement sent waves of pain through her shoulder, but she pushed forward, focusing on putting distance between herself and her pursuer.

She'd gone perhaps two hundred yards when the moaning grew louder. Three infected stumbled into view around a bend in the stream, drawn by the commotion of gunfire. Former hikers by their tattered outdoor gear, now reduced to shambling, virus-ravaged nightmares. Their milky eyes fixed on her movement, triggering their predatory instinct.

No choice now. She raised the shotgun with her good arm, bracing it awkwardly against her hip. The first blast caught the lead infected in the chest, knocking it backward into its companions. Before they could recover, she chambered another round and fired again, this time aiming for the head of the second infected. It collapsed, half its skull missing.

The third infected lunged forward, surprisingly fast. She tried to chamber another round, but her injured shoulder betrayed her. The shotgun slipped from her grip, falling into the shallow water.

With no time to retrieve it, she drew her survival knife. The infected crashed into her, its momentum driving them both backward into the stream. Frigid water closed over her head as bony fingers clawed at her face. She drove the knife upward through the soft underside of the infected's jaw, the blade penetrating into its brain.

The thing went limp, its weight pressing her further underwater. She struggled to push it off with one functional arm, her lungs beginning to burn. Just as dark spots appeared at the edges of her vision, she managed to roll the corpse aside.

She broke the surface, gasping for air, only to find herself staring down the barrel of Marcus's rifle.

"Quite a show," he said, standing on the bank ten feet away. Water dripped from his clothes; he'd used the stream to approach silently while she was fighting. "Almost worth the price of admission."

The shotgun lay in the shallow water near her knees. Her knife was still embedded in the infected's skull. She was weaponless, injured, half-drowned.

"Got to admit," Marcus continued, "you've lasted longer than most. Usually they're crying by now. Begging." His pale eyes gleamed with something beyond mere predatory instinct—a hunger that went deeper than survival. "But you're different. You understand the rules of this world."

The blood pounding in her ears nearly drowned out his words. Her mind raced, assessing options, calculating odds. The infected she'd shot would attract others. Time was against both of them.

"Here's what happens next," Marcus said, shifting his grip on the rifle. "You walk ahead of me back to camp. Try to run, I shoot out your kneecap. Try to fight, I do worse. Behave, and maybe I let you keep some dignity before the end."

A shadow moved behind Marcus—Eli, emerging from the tree line. The boy's face was flushed from exertion, his eyes darting nervously between her and his mentor.

"She shot two of them," Eli said, gesturing at the infected corpses. "Others will be coming."

"Then we'd better move quickly." Marcus kept the rifle trained on her as he tossed a length of cord to Eli. "Bind her hands. Behind her back."

As Eli waded cautiously into the stream, she gauged distances. The boy was nervous, not committed to violence like his mentor. A potential weakness. But with Marcus covering her with the rifle, any move would likely be her last.

Eli approached, cord in hand, clearly uncomfortable with his task. As he reached for her wrist, distant guttural moans echoed through the forest—the unmistakable sounds of infected drawn by the shotgun blasts.

Marcus's eyes flicked toward the sound for a fraction of a second. It was all the opening she needed.

In one explosive movement, she surged upward, grabbing Eli and spinning him between herself and Marcus. The boy yelped in surprise as she locked her good arm around his throat, using him as a shield.

"Let him go," Marcus snarled, rifle still raised but now unable to fire without hitting his protégé.

She began backing away, dragging Eli with her toward the fallen shotgun. The boy struggled weakly, more frightened than truly resistant.

"I said let him go!" Marcus roared, advancing a step.

She tightened her grip on Eli, eyes locked on Marcus. One more step backward. The shotgun was at her feet now. But retrieving it meant releasing Eli, exposing herself to Marcus's aim.

Another infected groan, closer now. Time running out for all of them.

Marcus seemed to realize the same thing. His expression shifted from rage to calculation. "Take the boy if you want," he said, his voice suddenly calm. "But the infected are coming. Neither of you will get far alone."

He lowered his rifle slightly. "We all walk out of here together. Deal with the infected. Then settle our differences afterward. Civilized."

A trap, obviously. But the approaching infected were real enough. She could hear them crashing through the underbrush upstream, drawn by the scent of blood and the echo of gunfire.

Making her decision, she shoved Eli hard toward Marcus. As the hunter instinctively moved to catch the boy, she dropped to one knee, scooping up the shotgun with her good arm.

Marcus recovered quickly, raising his rifle, but she was already rolling sideways as his shot kicked up water where she'd been. Coming up in a crouch, she fired the shotgun one-handed. The recoil sent daggers of pain through her injured shoulder, but the blast caught Marcus in the side, spinning him half around.

He didn't fall. Somehow, impossibly, he maintained his footing, turning back toward her with blood darkening his jacket. His face contorted with rage and pain as he worked the lever of his rifle.

She chambered another round and fired again, but her awkward position spoiled her aim. The shot went wide as Marcus returned fire, the bullet slicing a furrow across her ribs.

Both wounded, they stared at each other across fifteen feet of churning water. Eli cowered behind a rock, forgotten by both hunters.

The moment stretched, neither willing to fire again with infected closing in. Then Marcus smiled—a terrible, knowing expression.

"Another time," he said, backing toward the bank. "This isn't over."

She watched as he signaled to Eli. The boy scrambled after him as they disappeared into the treeline, heading upstream away from the approaching infected.

She wanted to pursue, to finish this. But the moaning was too close now, the splashing of multiple infected visible around the upstream bend. Her shoulder throbbed, blood seeped from her leg and side, and exhaustion threatened to overwhelm her.

Survival first. Revenge later.

Gathering her remaining strength, she moved downstream, putting distance between herself and the infected. The current helped, carrying her around a bend where a deer trail led away from the water. She followed it, pushing deeper into the forest, away from both infected and human predators.

Night fell as she found temporary sanctuary in the hollow base of a massive oak. The space was barely large enough for her to curl into, but its narrow opening made it defensible. She'd managed to relocate her shoulder—an agonizing process that left her drenched in sweat—and bandaged her leg and side using strips torn from her shirt.

The night air carried distant sounds—infected moaning, a screech owl, the rustle of nocturnal creatures. But no human sounds. No Marcus.

He was still out there. Hunting. Waiting. Perhaps as injured as she was, perhaps not.

Sleep came in fragments, her body demanding rest while her mind refused to surrender vigilance. Each time she drifted off, she jerked awake at some small sound, shotgun clutched in white-knuckled hands.

Dawn brought no comfort. Her wounds had stiffened overnight, limiting mobility. Fever threatened—not from infection but from exhaustion and exposure. She allowed herself two sips from her water bottle, a small piece of jerky, and five minutes to assess her situation.

Marcus knew these woods. Had the advantage of a partner. Likely had a better understanding of the infected zones. Her only edge was her willingness to do whatever necessary to survive.

She emerged from her shelter cautiously, scanning for any sign of pursuit. Nothing obvious, but that meant little with an adversary like Marcus. He wouldn't leave tracks unless he wanted to.

Setting a course away from the stream and the infected zone, she moved with deliberate care. Each step measured, each sound analyzed. She'd become the prey, but she refused to be helpless prey.

Midday found her on a rocky ridge overlooking a valley. Through gaps in the forest canopy, she spotted a thinning of trees about two miles distant—perhaps a road or power line cut. Civilization, or what remained of it, might offer resources or at least a change in terrain that could nullify some of Marcus's woodland advantage.

She'd just begun plotting a route when a flicker of movement caught her eye. In a clearing far below, a deer grazed cautiously. She watched its behavior, noting how it repeatedly raised its head to scent the air. Prey animal instincts. Like hers.

The deer suddenly tensed, then bolted—not randomly but directly away from something that had spooked it. Something it had detected downwind.

She didn't see Marcus. Didn't need to. The deer's behavior told her everything.

He was coming.

Abandoning her planned route, she moved laterally along the ridge, seeking better defensive ground. Her injuries slowed her, but she pushed through the pain. The rocky terrain provided less cover but would also hold fewer tracks. A calculated risk.

She'd traveled perhaps half a mile when the first shot struck. The bullet ricocheted off stone six inches from her foot. She dove behind an outcropping as a second shot chipped rock above her head.

"Impressed yet?" Marcus's voice called out, closer than she'd expected. "Two hundred yards, uphill, wounded, with a side wind. Still almost got you."

She didn't respond, scanning the slopes below for his position. Nothing. He'd fired and moved immediately.

"You cost me, you know," he continued, voice shifting position. "Six months setting up that cabin. Building a safe zone. Creating something in this hellscape. And you destroyed it in one night."

Another shot, from a different angle. The man was circling, keeping her pinned while closing the distance. She tracked his firing patterns, noting the rhythm of shots and pauses. Even with a skilled hunter's habit of topping off his ammunition when possible, he'd have to reload soon if he hadn't already .

"Eli thinks I should just kill you and be done with it." Marcus's voice moved again. "Boy doesn't understand the principle of the thing. Some offenses need to be answered properly."

She risked a glance around the edge of her cover. Movement caught her eye—a flicker of shadow against stone about a hundred yards below. Too obvious. A distraction.

The real attack came from her right. Marcus appeared from behind a boulder, much closer than she'd anticipated, rifle raised. She rolled as he fired, the bullet grazing her thigh as she tumbled behind a larger rock.

The shot pattern suggested he might be conserving ammunition. A potential advantage if she could force him to expend more rounds before making her move.

Seizing the moment, she leaned out, bringing the shotgun to bear. Marcus was already moving, zigzagging between cover as she fired. The range was extreme for a shotgun—the blast peppering the rocks around him but causing no serious damage.

"My turn," he called out, pausing behind a fallen tree.

She used the moment to shift position, moving higher up the ridge where larger boulders provided better cover. Her leg wound had reopened, leaving small blood droplets on the gray stone. No way to hide it now.

"I see you're bleeding again," Marcus observed, confirming her fear. His voice carried a predatory satisfaction. "Makes this simpler for me. Harder for you."

He was right. Blood loss and exertion were taking their toll. Her vision occasionally blurred, her movements growing less precise. Time was on his side.

A flash of movement to her left—Eli, scrambling between rocks, carrying what looked like Marcus's pack. The boy was being used to flank her while Marcus kept her attention. A classic hunting technique.

She had four shotgun shells left. Not enough to keep both at bay for long, and the noise would eventually draw infected even to this remote ridge. She needed to change the dynamic.

Moving quickly despite her injuries, she worked her way toward a narrow crevice between two massive boulders. The space was tight—barely wide enough for her to squeeze through —but it offered a chance. A confined space negated Marcus's rifle advantage and limited the directions from which they could approach.

As she neared the crevice, a suppressed shot found its mark, the bullet striking stone inches from her head. She ducked and rolled the final distance, wedging herself into the narrow gap. Small chunks of rock rained down as a second shot struck just above the opening.

"Cornered yourself," Marcus called out, his voice carrying an edge of triumph. "Bold move. Stupid, but bold."

From her position, she could see a narrow section of the slope. No sign of Marcus, but Eli was visible, moving cautiously from rock to rock, still carrying the pack. The boy's face was drawn with fear and exhaustion.

"Eli," Marcus's voice commanded, "circle around. Make sure there's no back exit to that little hidey-hole."

The boy complied, disappearing from her limited field of vision. She shifted, trying to cover both the main entrance and her back, where the crevice narrowed almost to nothing. A tight fit for even a child. But not impossible.

Minutes passed. The shadows lengthened as afternoon began its slow slide toward evening. Her wounds throbbed in time with her heartbeat, but she forced herself to remain alert, shotgun ready.

"Getting cold up here as the sun drops," Marcus observed conversationally. His voice seemed to come from directly outside the crevice entrance, though she couldn't see him. "You're injured. Bleeding. Exposure will finish what I started if you stay there all night."

He wasn't wrong. Hypothermia was a real threat at this elevation once darkness fell. But leaving cover meant facing his rifle.

"Tell you what," Marcus continued. "Surrender now, I'll make it quick. Clean shot. Better than you deserve, but I'm feeling generous."

She remained silent, conserving energy, assessing options. The crevice had seemed like a defensive position, but it had become a trap. Sometimes survival meant recognizing when a strategy had failed.

A new sound reached her—a faint scraping from the narrow rear section of the crevice. Eli, trying to access her position from behind. The space was too tight for him to bring a weapon to bear effectively, but his presence there eliminated her last escape route.

"Hear that?" Marcus said. "Boy's earning his keep. No way out now."

She could see parts of the crevice narrowing behind her, dust dislodged by Eli's efforts floating in the fading light. The boy was still several yards away, working his way through the tightest section, but he was making progress.

Marcus began whistling a tune—something old and vaguely familiar. The casual confidence in the sound was more terrifying than any threat. He knew he had her.

The shadows deepened. Her options dwindled with the light. Wait for darkness and try a desperate break? Hold position until Eli breached the rear of her shelter? Neither offered much hope.

Then she spotted it—a small depression in the rock floor near the crevice entrance. A natural channel, deepened by centuries of rainwater. And beside it, a fist-sized stone with one relatively flat edge.

An idea formed. Desperate, but better than waiting for death.

Working carefully to minimize noise, she removed her boot and sock. Using the knife, she cut a strip of fabric from her pant leg, then removed the remaining shotgun shells from her pocket. Three of the four shells she carefully extracted the gunpowder from, pouring it into the sock along with several small rocks. The fourth shell she kept separate.

"Getting awfully quiet in there," Marcus called out. "Not planning something foolish, I hope."

She ignored him, focusing on her task. Tying off the sock, she created a makeshift flash-bang—crude but effective at close range. Next, she used the strip of fabric to secure the single shotgun shell upright in the stone depression, primer down, precisely positioned.

Eli's scrabbling grew closer. Perhaps five yards away now. She shifted position slightly, anchoring her back against one stone wall and her boots against the other, creating a stable firing platform for the shotgun.

"Last chance," Marcus said, his voice hardening. "Surrender now or I'll have Eli flush you out the hard way. Boy's got a flare in that pack. Confined space like that, it'll cook you alive."

She took a deep breath, steadying herself. One chance. One desperate gamble.

In a single fluid movement, she took the flat stone and slammed it down onto the upright shotgun shell.

The explosion of the improvised shotgun shell filled the narrow crevice with deafening sound and acrid smoke. The flat rock she'd used as a hammer flew from her hand, splintered by the blast.

She barely registered the pain as she struck her knife against the rock near the gunpowder-filled sock, creating a spark that ignited the gunpowder fuse she'd fashioned from frayed fabric. In one fluid motion, she hurled the now-smoking makeshift distraction device toward the crevice entrance. It landed just outside, where Marcus would be positioned.

Not waiting to see the result, she raised the shotgun and fired her last shell toward Eli's approaching form at the rear of the crevice. The boy's scream echoed as debris and rock fragments struck him, forcing him to retreat. She was already moving, driving forward through the smoke toward the entrance.

The second flash outside the crevice—her improvised distraction burning in a bright flare—was accompanied by Marcus's howl. She burst from the narrow opening to find him staggering backward, temporarily blinded, his face lit up and hands raised defensively where he'd been caught by the sudden flash.

His rifle lay on the ground where he'd dropped it. She scooped it up, chambering a round as she leveled it at his head.

Marcus froze, his pale eyes widening in shock, then narrowing with hatred. "You can't—" he began.

Her shot dropped Marcus instantly. He crumpled, the back of his skull a ruined mass.

The silence hung suspended when she heard limping footsteps approaching. Eli burst into view, his young face contorted with pain and panic, holding his bloodied arm where the shotgun blast's ricochet had caught him. He froze at the sight of Marcus's body and the rifle in her hands.

"You killed him," he whispered.

She said nothing, simply watching as the boy processed what he was seeing. His hands shook as he raised his own rifle—too slowly, too tentatively.

"He was teaching me to survive," Eli said, voice cracking. "He said I needed to be hard to live in this world."

She remained motionless, the rifle still aimed at the ground.

"He found me after my parents died," the boy continued, words tumbling out now. "Said he'd protect me. And he did. He did! Even when he made me help with the others. The women. He said that's just how the world works now."

Tears streamed down Eli's face. "What am I supposed to do now?"

A flicker of something—pity, perhaps—crossed her face. She lowered the rifle completely.

For a moment, it seemed the boy might lower his weapon too. Then his expression hardened, transforming grief into rage.

"You ruined everything!" he shouted, finally raising his rifle with purpose.

She moved with the fluid grace of countless life-or-death encounters. Before his finger could tighten on the trigger, she had closed half the distance between them. The boy's eyes widened in shock as she deflected the rifle barrel upward with her left hand. His shot went wild as her right hand brought the knife up in a short, economical arc.

The blade sank into his chest with mechanical precision, angled upward toward the heart. Their eyes met as she guided his falling body to the ground, one hand still on the knife hilt.

"Please," he whispered, blood bubbling at his lips. "I don't want to be alone."

Something broke behind her eyes—a momentary fracture gave way to complete collapse of the carefully maintained wall separating survival from humanity. She held the boy as his breathing grew ragged, then stopped altogether.

She remained kneeling beside him long after his body went still. Her hands, steady through countless moments of violence, now trembled uncontrollably. A choked sob escaped her throat—the first sound of grief she'd allowed herself in longer than she could remember.

"Neither did I," she whispered to the boy who could no longer hear her.

Memories flooded back, no longer held at bay by the ruthless discipline of survival. She saw faces—her sister laughing in the sunlight, her father's proud smile, strangers who had shown kindness in the early days before the world completely unraveled. She remembered who she had been. A teacher. Someone who nurtured life rather than extinguished it.

The tears came then, hot and relentless. Not just for the boy, whose path might have been different in another world, but for all of them. For what humanity had become. For what she had become.

The sun continued its descent, painting the ridge in crimson and gold. The wind picked up, cold fingers finding the tears in her clothing, the wounds in her flesh. She welcomed the pain now, something real to anchor her as she allowed herself, just for these moments, to feel the full weight of everything lost.

From the valley below, the distant scream of an infected rose on the wind. The sound pulled her back to the present. Back to the reality of this world.

She gently laid Eli's body on the ground and closed his sightless eyes. "I'm sorry," she said, words meant for him and countless others. "I'm sorry we couldn't be better."

Slowly, she rose to her feet. Her shoulders straightened not with the mechanical precision of survival instinct, but with a renewed sense of purpose. The mask that slipped back into place carried something new—a humanity she'd thought long extinguished.

She searched the bodies with careful respect rather than cold efficiency. Each item she took—ammunition, water, medical supplies—represented not just her continued survival but a responsibility. To carry on. To remember. To find something more than mere existence.

Night would fall soon. The infected would grow bolder in darkness. Her injuries needed attention. The road she'd spotted earlier might lead somewhere worth finding.

She rose, swaying slightly before finding her balance. The rifle hung from her shoulder, its weight both burden and necessity. One foot in front of the other—not just the mechanical motion of survival, but steps toward whatever humanity might still exist in this broken world.

As she began her descent toward the valley, she paused to look back at the two bodies on the ridge. In another life, they might have been student and teacher, not predator and prey. The thought ached within her chest—a pain that proved she was still alive in ways that mattered.

Without further ceremony, she turned and continued down the slope, her silhouette sharp against the sunset until the forest swallowed her once more. But something had changed. She carried more than weapons and supplies now. She carried memory, grief, and the faintest ember of hope—dangerous things in a world with no horizon, but necessary for a journey that might someday lead beyond mere survival.

Afterword

The Unyielding Self in a Broken World

When I first envisioned the ravaged landscape of *No Horizon*, I was consciously stepping away from the well-trodden path of heroic narratives that often dominate post-apocalyptic fiction. The world I imagined, and the survivor at its center, were meant to reflect a more grounded, perhaps even uncomfortable, reality. *No Horizon: Survivor's Edge* has deliberately focused on the visceral, moment-to-moment struggle for existence through the eyes of an unnamed protagonist, a figure shaped not by inherent virtue or a destiny to save the world, but by the sheer force of will to endure in its ruins. In this afterword, I want to further explore the intricate, often paradoxical, psychology that has been both her greatest ally and her most formidable adversary

343

in this relentless fight for survival. Understanding this duality, I believe, is key to understanding the core of *No Horizon*.

The Double-Edged Sword of Survival

The protagonist's psychological makeup is undeniably a double-edged sword, a set of adaptations honed to a razor's edge by the brutal realities of the apocalypse. Her stoic and pragmatic nature has been her most reliable tool. We witness this unwavering practicality in countless instances: the almost clinical detachment with which she assesses the gruesome wound in her palm in *Blood Trail*, her calculated, step-by-step approach to securing shelter and treating the injury. This same stoicism allows her to formulate strategic ambushes against hostile survivors and dispatch the infected with cold efficiency, prioritizing survival over sentimentality. Her emotional detachment acts as a vital shield, protecting her from the debilitating effects of the pervasive fear, loss, and grief that define this world. Consider her largely internal reaction after her first human kill in the house robbery, or the almost matter-of-fact way she observes the deaths

344

of others, processing them not as personal tragedies but as tactical data. This ability to compartmentalize allows her to remain focused on immediate needs, a crucial element for longevity in such a precarious environment.

Furthermore, her resourcefulness and adaptability, born from the constant pressure to survive, are undeniable psychological strengths. She demonstrates a remarkable capacity to learn from every encounter, to improvise solutions with limited resources (like fashioning a Molotov cocktail or using dental floss for sutures), and to adjust her strategies in response to new threats and limitations. The teachings of Vex are absorbed and integrated into her skillset, highlighting her ability to learn and evolve within the confines of survival.

The Cost of Endurance

However, these very same survival mechanisms cast long shadows, creating inherent weaknesses that underscore the profound cost of her endurance. Her deep-seated distrust of others, a hard-earned lesson in a world where betrayal often lurks behind a veneer of desperation, fundamentally isolates her. While this suspicion has undoubtedly saved her from exploitation and violence on numerous occasions, it also erects impenetrable barriers, limiting potential alliances that could offer mutual benefit or shared burdens. Her initial wariness towards Thomas's family and her eventual, almost instinctive, return to the solitary existence that has defined her journey illustrate the profound impact of this ingrained distrust.

The emotional suppression that serves as an immediate survival tool may also be a long-term impediment, hindering any genuine possibility of healing or forming the kind of deep, reciprocal connections that can provide a sense of meaning beyond mere existence. The fear that she might indeed be "just like" Vex, capable of brutal pragmatism without remorse, suggests an internal awareness of the potential psychological cost of this emotional detachment. Moreover, her reliance on a "cold calculus"—a detached weighing of risks and benefits—while undeniably effective for problem-solving in critical situations, often leads to morally ambiguous decisions and carries the inherent risk of dehumanization. Her initial assessment of the family with solar panels, considering them primarily as a source of needed supplies, highlights the razor-thin line she walks between survival and a potentially corrosive pragmatism.

The Absence of Redemption

It is crucial to reiterate that *No Horizon: Survivor's Edge* deliberately steers clear of the conventional arc of the hero's journey. Our protagonist is not on a path of significant positive transformation. This narrative choice reflects a more sobering, but I believe more truthful, portrayal of how profound psychological trauma can leave lasting and unyielding effects on an individual. The cumulative weight of loss, violence, and constant threat can forge an identity so deeply rooted in survival that fundamental change becomes an almost insurmountable obstacle.

While the narrative does offer glimpses of a potential for something more—fleeting moments of connection with Riley, a hesitant act of empathy towards the sick raider, the raw grief and sense of responsibility following the deaths of Thomas and his family, the unexpected return to Crosswinds driven by a sense of obligation and perhaps something deeper—these instances do not ultimately signify a deep-seated shift in her core, survival-driven psychology. These flickers of humanity, though significant, are often swiftly extinguished by the overwhelming necessity of reverting to her detached, self-reliant state as an essential mechanism for continued existence. The pragmatic decision to leave Riley for the girl's own benefit, and her immediate return to the isolating familiarity of the road after the fall of Crosswinds, underscore the powerful and enduring pull of her survival instincts.

The Indelible Scars of Trauma

The reality, as I see it, is that the sheer intensity and prolonged duration of the trauma she has endured have likely created deeply entrenched psychological defenses that are absolutely essential for her continued navigation of this brutal world. These defenses, forged in countless life-or-death scenarios, become integral to her identity, resistant to easy unraveling. The constant vigilance, the ingrained distrust, the emotional barriers—these are not merely behavioral patterns; they are deeply ingrained psychological adaptations necessary for survival in a world stripped bare of safety and security. To expect a profound transformation would be to ignore the profound and lasting impact of such extreme experiences.

Survival as an Unyielding Endeavor

No Horizon: Survivor's Edge is fundamentally an exploration of survival as a relentless and often isolating endeavor, a journey where the landscape within is often as unforgiving as the world outside. Our protagonist's complex psychology, a potent and often contradictory blend of necessary detachment and lingering, carefully guarded humanity, serves as both her most vital asset and her most profound limitation in this desolate reality. Ultimately, these stories offer a glimpse into a truth that is often glossed over in more conventional narratives: that the scars of profound trauma can be indelible, and the arduous journey of survival may not always lead to redemption or a profound personal metamorphosis. Sometimes, the greatest

349

victory is simply to endure, unyielding, in a world that demands nothing less.

Thank you for venturing into this horizonless landscape. As you close this book, I invite you to reflect on the choices you might make in her place—and what those choices might reveal about the unyielding self within you.

—Ed Rodriguez